I0818731

a note on *a new land*

part 1

At Lower Farm, commune in Placitas, New Mexico, I ran into this guy who was sitting on the couch, sick, very hippiesque and open minded and open to all and welcoming, inviting me to join the movement, although I felt I was too old.

part 2

I wrote this here at home as almost everything else I've written. This during the growing presence of hippies here. I consider myself an observer, I thought, and still do think I was a bit young for the Beat Generation and too old for Hippies. It was amazing to observe the changes. At the time I was open to anything coming in to my mind and writing it down. In other words, I was a completely undisciplined poet, as I am to this day. History was irrelevant. Everything was the present coming in as I experienced it. I mention Gina and I mention Lee, two young women, and I mention Steve Katona, and Gino Sky who is a contemporary of mine. But primarily it is the flow of an acid consciousness, peyote consciousness, the result of the experiences certainly which were anything but daily and were rare. The room that I had at Major General Kenner Hertford's residence, since I was a caretaker there, had white walls and I turned it into a light show type area with a hanging lantern with a candle in it, just a coffee can with a bunch of holes knocked into it and it hung and floated around on a mobile and the light from the candle inside displayed all kinds of forms on the wall. And a light source towards hanging columns and strips of aluminum foil reflected changing patterns all over. I refer to that and many other things. It's a kind of a flow of my remembering what was going on then. Jumps are just part of my mind. -lg

dedicated to the memory of
Bobbie Louise Hawkens   Max Finstein
Kenneth Irby   Bill Pearlman   Stephen Rodefer
Kell Robertson   Mel and Beverly Buffington   Ann Quin

a new land

photograph by walter chappell

a new land
- (a voiced novel)
dried apricots
- (prose in a box)
prose fetishes
- (satirical trivia)
samurai dog biscuits
rodeo guts
- (fragments in a basket)

larry goodell

by the poet
Between Ann and Larry - 1965 to 1973 - letters with Ann Quin.
Making It (poems from 1968) - my poem making reproduced.
Dance Book (poetry and dance collaborations) - duende press 2023.
Escape, Grounded, & Commons - duende press 2020
Hot Art & Other Plays, 222 pp, duende press, 2019 - all the plays.
Nothing to Laugh About (poems 2015-2016), Pieces of Heart (poems 2014), Digital Remains (poems 2013), Broken Garden & The Unsaid Sings (poems 2011-2012), Beatlick Press 2015.
Here On Earth, 59 Sonnets, La Alameda Press, Alameda, NM, 1996.
Firecracker Soup, poems 1980-1987, 103pp, Cinco Puntos Press, 1990.
The Mad New Mexican (Songs 1981-86) Ubik Sound, 1986.
Online Publications - poetry articles blogs music - larrygoodell.com/ and duende.bandcamp.com/

CREDITS
Collage bird woman from a duende mimeo cover by Bobbie Creeley (contents page).
Some fragments from *Skylarks' Adoration Parlor* were published in *Chameleon 6,* One Shot Press, Albuquerque, 1982.
Tom Guralnick of Outpost Productions, collaboration using a Yamaha wind instrument, *Samurai Dog Biscuits,* premiered at the Living Batch Bookstore, Albuquerque.
Drawings for *Samurai Dog Biscuits* and *Rodeo Guts* by the author.
"Notes on Performance & Narrative Art" published in *Exquisite Corpse,* Vol.3/No.11-12/Nov-Dec 1985, page 8.
"Molson's Last Jerk" published in *Exquisite Corpse*, Vol. 2 No. 5-7 May-July 1984.
"Jane Russell, My Wife" published in *The Indian Rio Grande*, 1977.
Photograph of water and hands is by Walter Chappell.
Rooster snake watercolor by Lenore Goodell p 25.
Dried Apricots was written as a result of Stephen Rodefer's gift of a Japanese notebook plus two similar notebooks I made, typed and bound into booklets in a red & black box. Dec74-Apr75.
Lee Connor did choreography & dance to "The Written Work."

duende press
placitas, new mexico, usa
2019, 2023, 2024

contents

a new land

gift of Walter Chappell

1 Invitation to Change
2 Stars and My Little Casita
3 Around the Fire - New Buffalo Commune
Arroyo Hondo
4 Flower Child - Full Moon
5 Brother
6 She /for Judy Grahn
7 Peyote Meeting - Arroyo Hondo
8 The Blue Airplane
9 Chicken Dinner
10 Sun In Winter
11 Congressional Hearing
12 On The Mountain

12Jul67-11Mar68

1
INVITATION TO CHANGE

I was going to start a novel. Cosmic consciousness, he said, begins it and ends it. The rhythms that dare say anything at all come from the sides of the eyes. Beware. Have no *fear*. Rather, a stiffer riff must be blown. Working toward what pulls the pictures down from my walls. Masking tape won't hold. *Fall* with that. With anything.

I sit in a green womb chair. There is only love as far as I can see. This land allows a far look. A prophet spoke to me in dreams, came out of the wavy walls, the rock I stared at, cast out by divided consciousness. He lived out of dreams, sick on the couch, this Steve. Eyes electric, called him fabled prince. Bedecked in flesh.

"We love you. You won't go hungry." I wavered with the walls, the rug. Furniture. Equipment. Equipage. *Should* I join him. I prayed to the six directions. Flutter. A bird outside chirps.

2
STARS AND MY LITTLE CASITA

Star on the left palm. A thumb up your ass. A star is the last protection. Veils withdrawn. Hope to masturbate in the bathroom in the nut house. Can't. Everybody is watching. 2 minutes to pee? There is no straight line. A granite slab with my mother's name on it. Flat grass cemetery. Don't worry an inch. Star falls from my right thigh. Lace on the left. Worms hang out the left cuff. My T shirt. Stissing Lake Camps Staff. With a thunderbird. In blue.

"I will protect you." Bore the shadows of the leaves off the wall. The sun gone down. Or bore my stare into a boulder. Everything checks out. Turns. Waves. Sway back. And forth. Huge. Mushroom.

It is raining. Out the drain spout from the roof. Onto flagstones. Slight rain. Star up my ass. Left palm napalm village. Cluster. Smokes up from my thighs. Lace transfers. I will cover you with veils. Protect myself with changing hands. Left right. The slab swims. Bends sinks. I'm nauseated. That gone. I can't pee sometimes in 2 minutes. Stand there trying saying

I can't I can't thinking of people looking at me. COME OUT OF THERE. "Shake it more than 3 times and you're playing with it," the gay sergeant said to us in Basic. There's no stopping faces. Rain worms. Dragons. Stars. Faces. Thumbs. 2 minutes to pee. Countdown. Straight line. Dorothy Goodell. Mother. Lace on the left, lace on the right, get ready on the firing line. Cover you with protection.

Bends. Sinks. Aluminum foil takes on all the colors of the room. My light show projecting great arcs. Faces. The lamp with a red lamp shade. The innocents pull down their veils. Lift up their thighs. Poke their fingers in dirt. Pull off some leaves of mint. Keep the plant from flowering. It grows. Look down. Stars fall from my baggy T-shirt a friend gave to me. A sky-blue capsule. Acid. Placid. Drunk. Vertigo. Foil against the white wall. Plants in water. Plants in water. What are they, reeds?

The wind is not moving the geologic map of New Mexico hanging on the wall. It breathes. Swims. It is raining. Still come closer. Why do you talk so much. Everybody is talking. Please come here. There was almost a time to cry. The capsule. The grave. I am often banal. Blurt out. Inconsequences. Fingering strange plants, smoking. Yarrow. Pot. Asking about. Sacred datura. Lost in the spiral of a Hopi marriage mat. Kachina face in straw. Listening to the rain. The dog shaking his ears. Stars and thumbs. A limitation of time. Reverse. A and B. Matter and anti-matter all is nothing and something. Turning from their talking. I look. Stare. White-black transfer. Thighs itch. I dreamed we soaped each other's dicks and went off. He told me I am *innocent.* He chanted he was. Shouted into the aluminum foil. A dance with veils and detached memories. I sing to you in song. Tin Pan Alley rock and roll. Words lag behind. They are moving up.

I am lying on the slab. I am naked. I am the itch. Transfer. Stars on my hips. Thin legs. Stringy arms. Look. I rise swim. Rock. Go up then back down go up. Right. Left. Frozen. Boiling itch under my right arm. "I will protect you," that guy Steve said. Throw my arms around air. Dizzying. Height. Rock-bottom. I slide off the wall and float before, swing over and get down from the air wall. I love you
Steve star.
Steve star.
Steve star.
Lee, my first.
    Sun girl hair bare feet.

Lee.
Sun.

Gina looks off standing on the rock I stared at. Bore the shadows. Of the leaves. The light away. The sun did it. Gina. Lodestar. [Provider of the acid.] Protection of the left/right hole of light. Veil lace embroidery. The blouse Lee made. Homespun cotton. Flowers she embroidered around the sleeves. Stars. *Granite* slab. In a U shape. Floats over the ground. I swing on it. Shake it more than 3 times. Limitation of the reverse there is no reverse. Only forward. The right palm. Fingers are clothespins. Snap. Look into it. Look in to it. Steve #1 2 3 Lee Gina and on and on. Visions caught in my fingers, cups with things lit up crawling out.

Cups with things lit up crawling out. Ascend. The upward fingers. Down in dirt. Mint smell. It is raining. Gino. Sun love finger. Man. Mandala orgy. Wall face turns. Gino. Bearded sun lover finger man orgasm putty. Large eye written on. Solid orgasm putty. In the center of the eye. I rock you. Cup you. Tend to your thighs. Girl I plop down in. Only. Lee. Endless intricate patterns. Lace design you sent me in your letter. I look at. Lose myself. Self right left lost. Give up. Sway. Don't talk. Don't talk. Give up. Sway. I am my mother's death. Scriabin's Black Mass Sonata. Little fondling noises. Leading up. Without falling. Leading up I swing in the U-shape granite slab. Over the grass. It is raining. Through the cemetery. Over the town and the grasses. The plains. The mountains and up to here. It folds down away from me. The flagstone the water falls on. From the drainpipe. Stars from my T-shirt.

T- Shirt. A place I've never heard of on it. From Gino. Bends and sinks. I sit here in love with poets. And their lovers. Longhairs. Beardless. Palms exchanged. Search only for a lover. Unbend myself. My mind is permanently changed. Frontwards. Backwards. Peyote messages recalled. I will love in the clearing in the forest. Under the stars. Rain. Plant form. Water over every line that moves. Only forward where the rain follows a dry year. Hardly any snow. More than liquid. I will follow. The prophets lead my eyes. Into one. Blurt out. Silly, I'm to be trusted. The flat grass bends. Sinks. I am not lying down.

Words only are the voice. Voices to be trusted. In the shape of *thighs*. *Stars* over the belly. Man woman man. Woman. Come back to the protection of the innocents. The poet in the rain. His left hand up. Down. Rises. Protection of his images. Tongue is utterance down. Worms. Stars. Catch as can right and left. Ass fall marriage mat.

Gypsy star lover lost transfer. Rock. Dance dream messages grace the new beat. Wave out. Spore burst. Organ of deliverance. The center. And out the edgeless spiral. Tongue. Tongue. The skin is all I show. The gaping. Star flesh. And listen. It is to you. Potential that you hold him. Catch the changing hands, he is floating toward you. Center out center out. I come through you. THE BLINDING LIGHT IN LOVE.

3
AROUND THE FIRE - NEW BUFFALO COMMUNE ARROYO HONDO

What is in the fire is the help given to it. Major aims. There are too many faces to distinguish. Dear Max, poet, expert in mud. Thanks. Life in a carbolated petroleum jelly bottle is too much medicine. In the medicine cabinet.

There was so much fiddling with the fire. Damp wood. 'Chains on chains of conscious beings . . . who have no inherent form, but change according to their whim or the mind that sees them.' BEHIND THE VISIBLE. Yeats. On fairies. Poking fun at the fire. After a good meal outside. 10 miles from Taos on the Rio Hondo. Under for spacious skies. What happened to the kitchen gadgets.

Dear Jonathan. The loveliest. To prepare food for. What occupies the mind? The women wear skirts. And the men pants but not always, not always anything. Not even the fire.

We sat around. Friends and lovers. Sipped coffee. Smoked. A round of pot. Sacrament. To be inched up on. Community. To put in common. All the waiting and talking before you get on the land. The fire. Is the staring point for the coming in of spirits. Never too much alive to humiliate the departed. The hate gone out in death should have gone out in life. Rain. To the ground. These spirits are at ease. Ease. And stress. White Indians AmerIndians. Taos Indians invited them to their dances. An unusual act. These heepies. Who live in tepees. And take PEYOTL. Welcome. What work I could do. Helping lay the forms for the foundation. The sun house. Living center for winter. Kiva centered. A dome. Just the foundational lines. Visible from the tepees. Look in to where we have come to. The *meeting*. Work clusters. Not to get out of.

Or to get *in,* a privy with a view. MOUNT WHEELER. The scandalously beautiful rises of clouds. Voices everywhere, crops. Plans in the breathing. Up and down. Sit around. Mary and George, Joyce. Kids gone to bed.

Dear Lee. Why are you sitting there on Page Street. Stoned almost every hour. Love here. Behind the visible is the visible. Fanning the fire, the spark show. And I am alive. Bless. What is revealed. I see you glowing on that land. First hundred acres. Centuries before your minds will be ripe for despair.

DREAM

Sitting next to a couple at the firepit. There's a dance in town this evening. A *meeting.* An Indian lady walks up. Chants a peyote song. She holds the staff. Stands on one foot then another. She has long white hair. She rocks back and forth. Eyes closed as she chants.

She compliments Steve Kinny? who can chant *real good*. The man next to me offers me some peyote tea. 'Better take the rest of it.' I drink it quickly. He is sitting with his arms around me and his girl. 'I've got where I like the taste.' A long long time sitting before the firepit in perfect ease and warmth. It seems the warmth is our holding each other. Ourselves naked legs curled to ourselves touching. The cold feet warmed. He has to articulate it. And I say I love you. Surprised I said it. Then glad. Can't be any happier. Any other place.

We walk away. Questioning each other. 'Do you want to go to the dance?' I see his girl's face. Close. Small tattoos. Pink and blue flowers on her forehead and cheeks. They walk ahead. A fellow I'd seen weeks ago. Turns back to me 'I was just going to say hello. My God happy to see you'. He is blond, large. Cock-eyes. Smiles. We walk with our arms around each other and in tears. 'That's the way I said it would be — I'd see you when I see you. That's the way this place is. Turns out it's going to a dance.'

I don't want to relinquish it. Its aura is still with me.

✷

4
FLOWER CHILD - FULL MOON

The corpse I lay out is of old. Stones and ashes. This course I lay out is of old. Comparison of opposites. High to be free. Free to be there. Number to bed with. "It's a stone groove," Flower Child said, repeatedly. Moon. Glow. Stones to ashes. Number to be free. Lord God save my madness and your own peculiars. The hunchback over the skin. Flakes of the leper. Comparison of three. Combined. Combine. Fan. My legs are peeling. Interim: Nova Scotia. Moon in my madness. Flakes of ashes. Record albums left in the car somebody stole. *Lord bring me back my records.*

I don't want to be there. Moon madness. Drunk on Cottonwood. Total decline of the ancient voice. Voice *is* ancient. Voice 1 and 2 are no longer 3. Combination of stones. Your own peculiars. Have you a penny. To go to the store to be fed. Restore. The paint drops from my skin in pools. Of blue. Green on my back stays. I have a pipe you can smoke. Don't come up to see me unless you bring your own tobacco. Something in me said, said to a degree. I fight down old manners of speaking, living. I live. With my dry skin. Have you any virtue. I eat virtue. Smoke it. Tapers off in the hills. These are not large evergreen trees. Around me. Sorry I erected them. Take them down and put them further back on the stage. Flaked. Stones. High to be free.

I have never been to Nova Scotia. Nevertheless I am a religious man. Ne'er-do-well they called him. But he loved me. With his dirty hands. Bed to be free. Purity of our bodies. Embraced, embrace it. All around. Stones to ashes. He came up on his motorcycle. Flower Child. A beetle flew towards the light. I confused the two. Similar sounds. Sound. Me loving him. The corset in my closet. Will stay over a pool of blood. He lived in the middle of carefully selected things. Pardon me. *She* lived. We live there when we're over there. Carefully stepping between.

I will outline a new media. Madness. I think someone has put a hex on me. When they haven't. But I don't know. Have you any virtue in your basket. The difference between virtue. And *virtu*. Will remain in the dictionary for all to see when the time comes. Are *you* a good man? Don't you think that is a timely question? Why aren't we all marching around the room with the cats. Abbreviate disaster. Full moon and love all night. After he came down from acid and played the autoharp.

Rather spritely I'd say. Aren't we all strutters? But my objects are cleaner than yours and more carefully placed. Place me in your bed. That's right, just go ahead and pick me up. Before my colors. Peel off peel off and march together. With guns for totem poles or poles for guns. Are they still fighting over there? Ashes and rocks. A recent fire. The roof of the cave blackened, centuries of fire there. Clean out the rubble. See what I find. Shards on the ground. I'm looking for a whole pot to add to my collection.

The next time I saw you I noticed how dirty your ankles and wrists and hands were. You didn't smell in bed. A nice night indeed although nobody sat around reading any Dickens. He could be read of course. If somebody would sit down and do it. A lot of things could be done. More quietly, although it's better not to do them in secret. Unless there are 2 parties involved. There were last night. Although we all sat around together. The communal hippies on the floor, the non- communal hippies in chairs. I sat on the floor although I'm not part of the local commune. In the strictest newest sense. I resolved all the differences. Or thought I did. Lost some records. My billfold. It makes me mad, in fact. Who do they have living over there that they can't trust. In those communes.

I don't see things any clearer tonight. In fact, I'm a little nauseated. That is my line. Ashes to dust or whatever I've said. Cleansing cream and a helluva dick releases the pressure. Any known quantity can be combined. With another. Combination of 3. 4. You were good enough to love me. My pen needs filling. I will stop when the ink runs out. That isn't now. When my notebook is full. I write because I'm a living murder mystery without the murder. That isn't now. I took a shower. Put on my murder robe, did a Tarot reading. And I Ching reading. For you, Peace. You got. And the High Priestess. I suppose we can make love again. But your objects are so different from mine. The man we met on the road fixing his tailpipe was a freaky narcissist. With bags under his eyes, a magnificent chest. and tight pants. He stared visual circles around me. I went home and fingered my cunt. Cock, she said when she meant cunt. She called from the window, cock! Cock! It came running, on hi heels.

Smoke pot and listen to "Blonde on Blonde" the popular poet said to the society lady. She did. She just wanted to be hip. Felt strange and woke up from her usual dose of barbiturates and tranquillizers. With pains all over her body. I know her, she called me long distance and talked for almost an hour. My things are more easily seen from all sides. Than yours. Eyes lend usage. All those people staring in the new community on the other side of the hill. At things. Osage and usage. Letters not written. Things not done. I'm getting slower and slower. Ashes and diamonds. No diamonds. Ashes. The permission to scare up past cultures. Ask them how they did it. I am my own body. Corpse. Moonlight. What am I going to do with my life. Running out of time. Though generally happier, I can't groove with the community. Just an occasional member who hangs free. Flower Child. What am I going to do? He had wisps of hair sticking out from his magnificent build and his bald head was peeling. Other than that he worked well in a sex fantasy. In fact. I didn't care as I came.

"Are women objects to be used?" *Why* did you say that? The lesser known poet friend disturbed me more as time rolled by. The times were sexist. But I have a more careful selection than you. Though I don't have *Love* written on my pants. I'm not a cynic. I will glide. Pottery shards on the ground in front of the cave I found up in the canyon behind the house. Let's go up and explore and do freaky things there. Better be kind to the Indians, dead ones in particular.

My novel is progressing. My pen just won't run out of ink. Though it is increasingly scratchy in the prone position. Is everyone compelled to be funny at some time or another? Are we all an ego game? Go back where you came from, naughty word. Ashes and flower children. Evidence of past fires. I am a walking collage you can pick up and place where you wish. Now that requires some stretch of the imagination. I tried to keep from yawning. Over the phone. When she talked. So long. It's not very happy to be the only spur in somebody else's tedium. On the other hand tedium is not looking.

Outline your sanity. At what point does it break down. When nobody will give you an opening. I needed one. You said "please." The full moon. Choose to love. Love is so simple. A fantasy for wrinkled scrotums. Voice box. A sharing. We all took it off to get down to it. An old mistake in a new light. Crickets, moonlight. Up early hours writing. My life is falling apart it seems. Why am I good. Happy. But not well fed? Money problems. Hair problems. It all fits. The hunchback. I stand up straight and admit. I'm beautiful.

End it on a humble note. Is there that much ink left? Tired balls in itchy scrotums. A hallucination touched off from a perfect breast. Hey. Have you listened to "Sgt. Pepper." On acid? People sitting around not wondering what to do both when high and not high. Join up and move to the hills. Pepper the landscape. Erect your tents. Carry your flag poles. Under your clothes or no clothes. A slight nausea. A verbal vibration. Writing takes a lot out of him. Other than that, he's okay.

5
BROTHER

if the SUN were out
and it was night
we'd love alright
      say impossible?
open your arms
everything is mouth to mouth
trust to trust

Where we go from there is where we found ourselves the 1st time. An index of feeling. When you push out to love it rides the energy there and is no pretense that night. From all those people I come back up here. My lamp. The crickets outside. Do you understand. No city sounds. No one next door. Or upstairs. The dog asleep on the Navajo rug. Lightning. Diamonds. Rise and fall. Flight. Of natural wool black gray. White. Gray the color of death she said.

And black. Depression. My dog is black. Very few white hairs. All those people walking back and forth on this rug. Come in here. Temporarily. I am a figment of the past. Here on a cliff edge that is falling. I fall with it. My eyes snap colors in and out when I listen to ancient Indian music. And look at the lantern disk of colors in a wheel. On the wall. The first night. Catch me. Catch. Me.

A few heavenly blue morning glories this year and funny dry purple and white flowers. No crops up here. Abandoned fruit trees. Apricots too small to eat. Peach trees choked by the weed "heaven trees" grown up all over this place. The sourish grape vines. Growing haywire next to the arroyo. No one takes care. Or farms here. It doesn't fall but stays with the presences of men who lived here before Christ. Stalked these hills. Up in the canyon behind this house. Shot their prey. Camped in cliff bluffs. Shelters where the roofs are thick with black from their fires. Obsidian scrapers. Orange pottery shards. Arrowheads around in the earth. Fossils of marine life in rocks you pick up. It was all under water. Before the land uplifted into mountains

I have seen him walking in a dry place up there above. The shelter. Naked, I prayed. Felt his nakedness between the piñons and junipers. The long stiff-leaved bushes. Mormon's Tea. He with his own name for himself. Would have seen. And had his own names for. Heard him walking. The wind shaped the stream of my piss. Carrying my clothes, I walked down the slope of the hill. Dropped down the side a ways and saw the blackened rock roof. And later stumbling around trying to find it. I saw his face in the rocks beside the shelter. And later. After three years traveling the old road in and out of here. I saw floating in the canyon behind the house, his head. A feathered head. Looking out from the slate. Eye. Of the canyon. Where water still flows. I see the face now. The necessity of dealing with a fact. Excitement in encounter. Another person wants to live on the land. That is. What it says. Wants to build. A dome. Yes. And I do. Meet him. The presence guides me to himself. Turn in of structure. Circles within circles off. Center. Oil slick. The mind. Body adjunct. Controls. Rolls out before my eyes from somewhere. Before them.

He wants that fact of encounter and I do. To do it together. Seeing ourselves in it. That it is the beads. Their own material beauty. Not that *he* or *she* strung them. In lines their own hanging. What is all this of the eyes and ears. The stronger need. To look in to. Look in to you as I listen to Missa Luba, the drums and the black voices. It is well. Exciting. Ex sighting. Sighting it stoned together doing it. It is the rush of colors given from what is thrown on the white wall. Back. Eyes lessen them. Dulled but to snap back full. Brilliance. As I listen.

Give myself in cross-legged sitting position. Over. I am the energy that is out of waves my body is making and breaking. Getting rid of is subject to. Greeted in tiredness. By closed-eye vision. When least expected. Snap out and sway. Change flashes, the store of all triangles of my being. Made pyramids. Made cylindrical. Hexagrams. Floating. 6-sided plates, some with holes in them. It is not to be put down in words easily. Or even at all. It is gift of walking. Men who lived here and hunted. Farmed. Pottery and clothes the women made. The chants that allow the inner coilings to vibrate. The chants. Chanting allows this to be so. We come into this and it is a young friend I direct this to. Speaking aloud as my pen moves across the notebook pages. I am prompted. To say. Said to be prompted. Urged. On. In bare feet. Levis, old purple shirt. Blue bead string around my neck and black and white beaded necklace too. Given to me. By friends and a pink button you gave me. Over the heart. Cross in a flaming heart. 8-spoked wheel out from it. Take a Trip. With Creator.

*

There is a gap between the men I feel the presences of stirring in me. And. Who am I. That my grandparents came from Illinois, Texas, Kansas. Kansas. They were farmers then barbers and restaurant men. Then business men. That is dealing with papers. That have to do with money. My parents, insurance salesman. And. New suits of good quality factory-made material. Material of. Dirt on the soles of my feet I've walked in so many classrooms. In shoes to go on from that paper business. Some higher form. Of insurance. That is, a profession.

Teaching, it began to turn out I taught. 3 years. Boys from 12 to 17. A few came up to see me yesterday. And we were all talking about the same things. And they were interested in what they have given me. Writing poems. Going to San Francisco, going now. To college. How many ways can you spell. Fuck. A recording we talked about. Of all the ways it is said in this room. You and I have. What we give to each other in our taking from each other. I am not a teacher. I am falling back from my age, 32. To where you are taking me. I want it. What is mine must fall through my fingers and pile up underneath. Not gold, dirt. To go in to. Do what with? Make sounds. Feel the cool earth.

You are the presence that I'm permitted to feel. The sun and moon permit. Beyond them, the planets. Beyond them, stars. Beyond them (the weights and gasses). Other galaxies, whatever patterns transmit. Are in fact *telecast* to me. I see you in them. Walking or just. Asking for a cigaret, or just playing the autoharp as you do well. And singing "Everybody said they was his friend. They all said they wanted to see him come back again. But they didn't know jus' exactly when." It is not just your song. It presents itself through you as you play and sing it. All is part of space and the time sings. Hard to see anything clearly without looking at it. I let fall what must. *Say*, be said and done with. There is no correction.

I copied down "a reconsideration of our position as insignificant germs. On a minute ball of rock attached to a minor star. On the outer fringe of one of the smaller galaxies." To go out in a spiral without losing center requires some understanding of the six points. They. Hover over the rock hill I go out to. To pray. And greet me. Each way I turn. In their directions I am coming closer to you. Your. Youth. I am. Needing. You. A reconsideration of our position. In lieu of circumstances. Beyond our control.

Will the center ever find itself?
It transcends all. Definitions of God. A stone groove. A tablet. Of love. Two human beings. Weave in and out. Of each other's life. Will the center ever find itself. You draw me. Toward you. God is the only twin life has. A stone. Groove. The race is divided in halves. Male and female are in each of us. I follow you then turn back here. Where the only distraction is the flow of uninterrupted sounds – spring water falling into the pool outside. Crickets again, and the dog.

I refuse all colors but gray. And in that I see the growth of the lamb. Sheep's wool. Variegated. Hand spun. Hand woven. The simplicity of this rug my feet touch. Is endless. And in that we can set up our own controls. You write a new song and I go out by myself. To see in this simplicity. I rest on the fires that are given to me. In ease the thoughts weave themselves. Into oblivion. Or into. I cannot think about it. Because there is no thinking where we are led. To come back from and go up. Or out, our bodies. Our shelter and the food we grow. Cook. And eat. I can open myself. As you yourself. To what endlessness is there. Strike out 'is.' The love I walk back with to give you. Closes the gap. A beginning. You are the one. Who floats and draws me here. And you change so that you take me. Where I go. Wherever I meet you.

6
SHE

She is the one. Only. Draw out of my fire. Come to me in two women. In the morning the large one is feminine. Sun through her silk house dress. Short hair looks graying. But she's in her mid-20's. The small one looks like a little boy. "I come to you in the guise of a boy." Girl woman. A man's little brother she was. Bounced around. Bells on her boots. A fairy woman. Puck. Tom Bombadil. "I come to you. As an old woman. Sitting in a chair. A rocking chair. I am reading you. My portraits. Of famous people. Recognize me. I am one. Or the two. Who approach you changing their clothes. Shapes. Over the hill. The *green* hill. I am short. And heavy. And my brother is well-built. You can't even dent his thighs. You are exercising. You look at your arms. In the mirror. What do you see. Why again why are you. So thin." Thin mother. Father. It's in. The line. "I come to you in design. *Trust*. Run the rampant way out to the end. And decide *what* I say.

"One time I jumped out of a Holiday magazine and you couldn't take your eyes off me. You hung me above your desk and called me. Languid Lady. Eyes down on the drink I am not touching. My hair. Golden-brown. Every which-a-way in the sun I call you Larry. Larry without looking up. Or there is something mysterious about my heavy eyebrows. Or is it my chin. Too prominent. That makes my eyes look uncomfortably slanted. My hair was long. You took me for a long ride. You mention me in poems. But you avoid me. I divide. Watch out. I am surrounding you. Try to catch me with your pen. You can't. Your voice. *Your* voice. Don't ever speak to me. Wait till you're spoken to. Don't listen for my car. It isn't my car and it isn't coming up to your place. It isn't. Your place. And anybody who loves you loves you from a distance. Alright complain. But not to me, to your other gods. I am two identical women. Listen to me. I cover the floor. The walls are women. The ceiling, my sliding. Faces. Hair down in the bed you. Ran your hand between the strands. How do you manage it. That long hair. In bed lying with me. Your visions.

"Do you remember your visions? You were touching the pectorals of a Roman soldier. Do you think I didn't know? I sent you fields of poppies. Fields. Of spices too many to name. And finally. You managed to fuck me. Never mind what I was going through. One of the first things you asked. And lying with me and it was okay. and you got up and wrote for it all. WOMB OF ALL MESSAGES — FLOWER OF THE EVENING SONG.

"Thank you. We have our arms around you. *My* hair is close cropped. My legs rather heavy now. I am *we* all along. We hold hands and dance around you. Don't look for light in the fire. Take *me*. Take *me*. You bastard. Innocence innocence. That passes. You are too *good* for me? We go. Around we go. Faster. You know where it ends. Taking stepping. Take a stepping. Step the ritual taking. Go-ward go-ward, tones off. So fast. The flutter flurry dash around. Skirts off legs around you. Breasts blur. Breasts. Arms kiss now in air. Stream of kisses. Kiss now. Play around. The air play. Whiz of whir gone. Dozens of us lip your ears. Kiss in there. Down the cones, the throat. Cough. Pull out? Bang we bang you. Fall. Fall you are simply. Coming out of it. On the floor – bed – chair. Do you remember your visions. A whir. Over you. Vanished wings. Don't think about it. We have. Gone into you. Gone. To come into. You. You are reception for us. We gang up when we choose. Cannot avoid us. Give you. Strange bouquets. Very small. Remain what they are. Even when the water dries up. In a blue glass. Long spurs of seeds. The grasses. Verbenas, paper white flowers. And always. We leave you many yellow flowers there are no names for. Or if you look for them you will. Destroy. Suck. The air. After I am gone. I come driving down. On you. Change. Is the sex in my mouth. Change. Is what I wear. Am outside of. I come to you naked to tease you. Called me. Temple Dancer. Ha! Here you are the old man, little boy. And I the old woman, young girl. I am you. For an instant. Instant favor and my brother stands behind me. In golden armor. He doesn't have a whip. Though you might see him holding it. He will protect himself. From your advances. Your wanting to be him safe from me. Knowing *we* don't make love. *Look.* I am much lighter. It is late at night. You are here by yourself, you thought. So much self-pity and then I stepped outside you. I danced around long before you saw me. And the bells are ringing as my feet hit the floor. But my flesh pulls against itself. The heavy one is in me tonight. And she keeps me from bouncing far. Off the ground change.

"Don't ever take me for my brother. The flames of your head. Run out. Give in when they do. I'm all you ever met. Need to. Don't ever take me for my brother. He has his job. Doesn't involve you as much as you sometimes think. Don't write so fast, listen. I am as strong as he is. I am slowing down now to show you. There's something of love here. But I won't favor you that far yet. Probably never. If I were a lion you would not throw rocks at me. And for that. I love you a little. The late evening when you are alone. Moths banging against the window. You've been listening for hours to church music. Written in Shakespeare's time ha! The presumption! Peel it off. Peel. It off. My wings now rub your shoulders. You incompetent. Do you really believe they do? You do. Then I'll leave you to fabricate more things if you wish. They're only words without an ounce of meaning. You see. Without anything. The dull weight of words. I leave you. See, you haven't anything more to say now."

7
PEYOTE MEETING- ARROYO HONDO

Suddenly things are warmer and drawn up closer. A woman that is in every way something to come to.

"The trees
Of some dark forest where we wander amazed at the selves of ourselves.
Stumbling. Roots stay." - Jack Spicer

The wanderer that was given a name to call his own couldn't find it. He looked in the nest at the base of the tree, couldn't find it. A blue-green egg and 3 yellow ones. A black banded bird flying about cackling. And sucking noises from a bush. Lips that are hearts in a bush. Draw me down I am struck from behind. The trees fall in. The magpie folds its wings. Falls dead. Downward *I* fall. The glass floor. I slide. To a stop. A princess who is very tall stands in the center of the floor.

There is no center. Walls won't give in to any recognizable structure. Limitation drops like weights from her mouth. Down on me. Limitation limitation. A mild 'Fuck You.' Or is it very loud shakes. The glass walls. Her hair is of course golden. My colors are black and white. She knows they are not painted on but grow from me like the fur of a skunk. Not that I would want to be any place else. The presence informs me. Who *I* am. Where there is an echo under the I. Ever losing its foundation. So I cannot say anything to her beyond a stumble.

I am brought to her through the sucking bush of hearts, the fallen nest of eggs. The magpie which strikes me and I become, falling crosses for eyes. I'll see you in the comic strips.

Open the page and try to find an A. There is no order except what comes before. (It is given.)

I am a neglected child found in the rain by 4 turtles who dragged me back into the water and raised me on oysters. Other than that I was born in a Bircher town. Where a wild moon drew just as powerfully. A bunch of crazy men. Crazy after money. Awash on a sea when everything was desert. Listen. I am sprung up in no definition. But a griffin holds a candle on the table. And I light the candle. "A transition from self-glorifying artistry to voluntary devotion toward the community."

There is a fire.

> The stone which the builders rejected
> The same was made the head of the corner:
> This was from the Lord,
> And it is marvelous in our eyes.

Peyote Woman is the Pole Star. Lode Star. Fire. Star Fire Energy. Source. Where the wind collects the particles an earth is born if there is no wind. A fool is born. Listen. The glistening sun through leaves in the door and across the rug. The candle burning. And the Sadhu priest cross-legged on the wall. All the coverage that is here is there. Is here is there.

She brought the pail of water in. Sat on her haunches before it, lit the tobacco and said a prayer over it. Peyote Woman, I was in a field of eyes. Brilliant golden CBS eyes. Hundreds. Everything multiplied in my visions that night. The floor of the tepee was glass. And the Princess was the fire. The Earth Woman before her passed the pail of water to us. We passed it around and drank. Water. Sage. Cedar. Cottonwood. Cottonwood only is used for the fire. The coals raked back in a crescent before the "road." Cedar bark on them. And the smell of cedar rises through the tepee.

The Princess flickers through the broken lines. Receptive Earth Woman are her borders. The sun dims. And I have received a call from her lover who, like me, is incompetent. The glistening jet streaks by, all the machinery of a colder mind at its controls, given that as predominant masculine force. The Devil has reason to laugh. Assume the form of the Princess. And laugh at me from the fire. Still. I worship on a corner of land given to a community. For strength to finish. The 1st building. And for strength against the sickness. Evil thrown out from the Devil's flies. Shit. Food. A meeting was held. Sage smoke before me. I inhaled the leaves deeply when a wave of nausea came from the buttons I ate. And the tea I drank. Peyote Woman swims to me from the pail of water. The first to greet me. And her lover. We are a ring of lovers. Rejected stones. Wanting to touch out over the fire.

I do not represent any formal occasion. Only the ceremony with gourd and voice and water drum. Turns itself in my mind. 2 strands of smoke spiral up. And the fire. Is a color all its own.

Where else to go. It is all within. I love you. Not vainly believe. Give up to the only illusion. The gold from the italic point of my pen reflects the sun as I write. Into my eyes. Commune.

I will come to you. Who are me. Blind me as I write. Who ever thought paper was flat. That anything was straight at the base of everything. The candle burning down. Is the blue bus. White Swan Laundry Bus. All blue. And white. The swan will bite you and fart. Alter ego of Gemini is Pisces. I am Gemini. She is Pisces. Earth Woman. Would bring the water to me if she could. We will have a peyote meeting once a month. There is so much work to be done. We need strength together. Men working women cooking. Children back and forth. and other times we go up on the mesa. Take acid together. No formalized anything. Fits it. The quick way to the old things. But enough is enough. For too many and more and more. It's a cap of "freaky franticness" "guilt-exacerbating anguishes *or* almost unnatural feverish ecstasies." From a letter from a friend had enough. And wants the plant. The woman brought back to her tribe. And renewed them. As it renewed herself.

⁕

I will dance around this fire. I will sing the song of young people doing something with the Indians' elements. On that land high on that land. Beyond that are city towers rotting in their own cement, the cement Devil who would devour the Princess in the fire. Were it not for the chants that continue all night. Those that know them. Those picking them up. Give us strength.

I will not see you many times again in your plush house. Young man and woman. Blind to the urges of your own ages. The renewing is taking place and you make me feel young again. You. Come home. In your comfortable. Stylish way. With packages. and packages from the biggest shopping center. The kids scream and have their way. Love. Something says. No thinking. Only the giving in. To the strength there. Resting again. On that fire.

Listen. I am at loss for a lover. Fire woman I can't touch. The other with her own. No possession. But the possession of the tongue. When you can't stop it. Even if you try. The guru on the wall behind the burning candle. Is beyond me. My course is limitation dropped from the lips of the Princess. The light from the window is sun through leaves. Holy spectrum given in late afternoon. Friendship is renewing. And can be a lover. Come unexpectedly out of the meeting of forces. To play. Bear on it. I am the dark forest as everybody knows. Everybody is. Who rides. The corner of the fire. And goes where it goes. All the basics meet in a beginning. All four aces of the Tarot. Came up. I am led on. To less deceiving. Patience to give in. The fires are never mine. The direction is a toss up. The moment is used without knowing. It is used. The bottom of the glass. Is endless to look through. And the city there. Dissolves into the sun.

8
THE BLUE AIRPLANE

A blue airplane. Do you think you can reach it with that? Be clear come to grips with it. The leaps are too frequent. I pull the stick back. And the plane lifts toward the sun. I am the sole pilot and can you only believe it. There is no symbol here only the stick I pull back. And the plane goes anywhere I wish. The blinding light.

*

What I wouldn't give to live with them. All of them spread this warmth out. That gags me now. Tears. Wash my face. Suicide. I drive it. While I go on down there on Earth. Lift up engine strains. Into the heat. That I will go on living down there. Revolving around. Nearer to this, I do it. Heat dries my tears. The sun is oval from close up. Oval I drive into drive into. The plane is my own. Architecture. Heavy drone like a boat now. As if I'm going down. Down storms around me. Going down. Fire in my face. Let go the stick forward. The plunge. Storm fire. Explosion. O God I carry them all with me.

*

A blue airplane. Reaches. Where the outside of the mind meets the inside of it. Gets you there. Gets you across when it is too far to jump. I know it is difficult. On the other hand, you are relaxed. As you want to be. That opening you are entering, whether you see yourself there or not. Because it is pleasurable, can be returned to. More and more. By letting go at the last.

*

I carry a model of the blue airplane. Now that I've destroyed myself. The last channel of self-pity. Taking them all with me, walk the Earth now. The sole survivor of an unknown suicide Pact with the Sun. Spread this warmth out. Lift yourself and go. To the garden of no symbols where the riches of Paradise grow.

Come back. Come back. Solitude. The unanswered question. Loneliness brought me. To the palace of the Sun King. A yellow flash. And the airplane was a skeleton around me. Saw it at once. As its own death. Separate from me. Although you can say it got me there.

The never-ending steps. Through the towers of the Sun-Flames. Towers of the Sun-Flames. Sun-Flames. All the arches of paradise before me to infinity. The colors of the rainbow and I am at the door.

Entered through. The great disk of shells turquoise red-stone white-shell abalone-shell cascading shells the bright lights from each disk beyond disk beyond disk not allowed to see. Progresses before me as I am drawn on on. Upside-down face, red and yellow forehead, lower part of face green. Pautiwa, Sun-King upside-down, rises back burning from me. Fire-feathers radiating out in a spin, rattles and a flute playing. I am led to the left, a rascally guy playing the flute. Yellow butterflies coming out of it, then blue-green, red, white, black. Then all-colors butterfly. I follow. Dances and I dance. Tell me to dance. Hands burning, lips chapped. Fire-yellow. Flame origin everywhere, I step as it steps and follow. I flutter.

My wings are multi-colored I become. And the maidens are dancing around me with nothing to do but taunt me. The winter months are here. Dancing around me. 7 or 8. I lose count. I flutter to the bright wall and land there. They bunch up and look at me. Talk to me. The evil sisters. Coo to me. Oh! want to copy my designs. The split-black pupils on my wings they love. Set in changing turquoise. Eyes that are wings stare back at my evil sisters. O where are the *good* maidens, the 7 other sisters? Sleeping through the winter. The fiery faces get so near I fly off. Dip flutter, they throw things at me. Clothes. Fly off them. At me. I *rise* fall flitflit. Mantles sashes try to net me. I fly burning multi-colored crazy *running* after me. I flutter higher. Look down, they are naked under me. And the maidens are exhausted. Disks of shells. Rattle on the walls. The burning center face that was watching. Father-brother laughs. Pautiwa. The serious one. Yellow green and red one in sun heaven flaming out. Wonders what I'll do, his sometime brother-lover. I am the clown. Fluttering down now over the naked sleeping maidens.

Ha! I step out of my butterfly disguise and blow upon my flute with burning breath and ha. *Kee!* They turn into crazy butterflies, the 7 evil sister butterflies and Pautiwa laughs. I jump up and down and all the great shell disks on the walls rattle and shake. Sparks shower out. And masks after masks come out of the baked mud niches. And rattle and shake and laugh. And the 7 crazy butterflies. Fly weird loops. Sex-crazed butterflies. Fly about. And the good maidens in the opposite chambers laugh in their sleep. Pautiwa, with fire-thrust tower flame, sends the sister butterflies out to the 4 directions. To bring rain. And I am told I am hidden. From the eyes of men. Unless I go back where I was. Renewed in the changing flight. Everything both ways. And he will bring the spirits of the good maidens down. To Earth. In turning-back moon. December. Their flesh will come down. To be planted. They will become matrons in the growth. And dance. Dance with them in hand.

⁕

I carried only me. Back. To those I somehow live with, wanting to be closer. The community of the love-lost-gained. I ride back to the land. With the outside-having-come-into-me feeling. The plane left behind. No longer needed on this ride. From the flame towers back. To the mesa country. Butterflies come from my flute. As I play. And the rays. Vibrate and breathe. As I ride down from the sun –

"Be neither too shy, if you are a plant
nor too bold, if you are human
for we are the same essence. We
work together to produce. The life flesh.

Almost obscured. Suicided suicided
by desperate mechanical flights
I will overload your senses.
You would never have thought there was so much.
It rains down. In your return. The dancing sisters come
the colors of corn. Grains.
Even after the herdsman murdered the farmer
you few dance to the butterfly maidens
and make them bear as you build and plant again
mud bricks laid. Water over the hands
the universe, galactic voices in and out. Meet
water over the hands. Life Flesh
the garden you plant. Among the evil faces
is the riches of youth. They would copy your designs
in *backhand.* And kill you with them.
There is *only* the return. And the Paradise you give
from the sun that *burns* of its own. Unforced
within you."

9
CHICKEN DINNER

Water over the hands. Moment of recovery! *Down*. Is it lost? Question. You could be a rag doll, she said to her little girl but then you couldn't talk or eat or poop. The bongo player leaned forward. Not to poop would be the only bad thing.

We waited an extra hour or so for the dead hen to cook. The dog had got it the day before. Biscuit-Eater you can call the dog now. Chicken killer. The bongo player asked if he was too loud. No. Went on playing. Then I put on a tape of a song I'd just written. Me playing a Cochiti drum. With different sized sleigh bells tied to my legs. Stomping on the floor as I sang

> steel-bent mish-mash stranger jockeys
> low in the saddle we ride (muse come to me)
> float out over the countryside (boom boom boom)
> countryside . . . .

Death came to me in the cards. Music of Heinrich Schűtz on now as I speak, speak of the mind. Everything pinned on the High Priestess. She guides me. I, reclining on my mother's afghan come to me after her death. Mouth, the sacred dwelling place of the word. Do not reverse this woman. Drastic midnight curtains come down around me. I am in the middle of the stage swallowed up by its trappings.

Come to me, *Death* in the organ music, Heinrich Schűtz. There is only the candle of imagery to burn. And piñon incense, the real thing. The fragrant aroma of small-town firewood that is characteristic of the season. Sipapu, a source, and way above, the burst out spirits inflated everywhere and billowing down on me. I escape to the foothills of the Rockies. Bounce back to the foothills of the Sandias on the tip of the slide. Mother, I give in. Don't block me. The fingers are the internal game of make believe you're attached. Are you?

I've had my first poem published in WORLD 8. That's what's going on in New York while I breathe piñon incense here. Personal jack-off. *All jack-offs are personal*. Be quiet.

> Steel-bent strangers mish-mash jockeys
> leading the way where we go
> float out over the countryside, moving slow . . . .

Moving slow. The chicken finally got done after we were zonked on tequila margaritas and ready. A good bird there dead cooked on the plate.

A candle burning. 4 people lost in separate commitments. He is occasionally/all the time? committed to her. She *more* to him. The other guy plays bongos and is mystery man in this community. I, as usual, am a visitor tolerated as a special guest. Come and go. Mostly go. Weighing the inner and outer *violence*. Which is stronger? Look at each other and wonder what each other's mysterious pasts have been. Going forward now. The need to *knock* out a few lamps. Turn over a few things, pull the curtain rod down, part of the wall crumbling behind it. *Adobe*. Everything is mud. Tearing a handkerchief in two. Gassing the toilet. Poking acorns with needles and stringing them around somebody's neck. Looking up an old friend you can't get along with any more just for an evening of put-downs. Drinking together hoping somebody *else* will get in a fight and you can watch. Cussing the bulls out for being cowardly at bullfights you've never been to. Sucking the world *in* till everything wrinkles. The seas fall off. It's all a big cunt you can't even fuck. Read about it and finger your hallucinated dick. The dickless mob arrives for their first lesson in robot maintenance. *Don't want anybody fucking the machines*. Oh golly gee whiz. In a *tank* rumbling down a highway and have to piss. And we'll fall off into a chasm. It was all predicted. So I tell you

join the jockeys stranger women
deep in the saddle we ride
move out over the countryside, countryside . . . .

Back to my chicken dinner and the story of football. This is U.P.I. The machine just took over my voice. Types on to Schűtz's music. Some knob down there was wrenched too far. *Popped* the circuits. I'm giving you popped circuits just a few weeks before Christmas. The new craze for Santa Claus's brassiere. Dancing in drag in a dark private club in Dallas. Back to the chicken dinner. It was good and the company tip-top. A young poet from New York and his chick talked back and forth, the country slap-dang-doodle. A game with cellophane balls for words. Bandied things around. Is there a real sex-love under all this?

The chicken and the sweet potatoes and dumplings and Sauterne were all good. And the big mandala sheet hanging on the wall floated in candlelight. You pick up a sheet in the middle. Tie it with string several places. And dip it into dyes. Let it dry and spread it out. We learn to pass on. *Ate* the chicken. Mother, I'm dead. I'm not what your son thought he ought to be. Ought he thought to be? Flip-flap. How it all began.

*

"Sim" the Robot does almost everything. Except say *ouch*. A marvelous mechanical man, says LIFE. *Simulates* a real patient in almost every respect. Controlled by a computer. Can even throw and catch a football. And recite its history: In 1863, Cornell had taken up football and so had the University of Michigan. Plans were laid for a game between the two. Nothing I say is my own. The dummy's amazingly lifelike eyes not only open and close realistically but the pupils also dilate (above left). And contract (above right). Plans were laid for a game between the two. On the Day of Pentecost the apostles seemed to go barmy. They spoke in tongues. People said, are these men drunk? Cornell's president cancelled the game with these words: I will not permit 30 men to travel 400 miles merely to agitate a bag of wind. Peter said, "Well, it's only nine o'clock in the morning. We could hardly be drunk yet even if we were drunkards." Future "Sims" will bleed, perspire, salivate and turn blue when short of oxygen. Look at his eyes at any length and you will begin to go mad. The modern football game began with a confrontation between two 11-man teams, Harvard and McGill, in 1874. They *all* stopped working. Those that owned property sold it and divided up the money among the community. The clash resulted in a scoreless tie.

Back to back, we scratched each other's backs. And did other things without getting under the covers. We carried it on well undercover. *Hippies are those who've had so much cake they're sickened of it.* Oh bells bells and drums. Things I can't eat or put on. Fancy the inward road.

Stranger jockeys
deep in the saddle we ride
float out over the countryside
    (boom boom) . . . .

Tons of mud in the walls. Skies that knock you over. *Here* it is towards the 4-corners area. And down around here chants sent back and forth in letters. Give me a *good* chicken. What we had wasn't just a dinner, a *together* dinner. Transplanting of roads is found in every human being, if you can only draw it out. Urge from the balls, what glands. Helps to draw it out. I love/sex you. Feel-urge. Splat magic. Dope hinterlands. Smile and mercy magic. Rubadub. 3 men in a tub playing the tuba. Passing it around like a third eye. The road over. The baker's cake. I won't screw. I want to *bury* myself in *cake. Take your prick home.*

She danced in from the sunflower field and announced she was originally from Kansas. Well *hell,* good God a lot of us are. Then the head man lowered the velveteen curtains over us and I fumbled with her ballet dress. We shouted at each other whether poetry was dead or alive as we fumbled. The audience out front was made up of retired bakers. Pat a cake pat a cake baker's man. Have you any wool? 3 pails full. I fingered her funny bra. Her beard kept getting in the way. "I'm too fat she said, and roly-poly jello? That's better than cake.

Boos from the audience. *We want violence.* They start beating each other up into batter as Mary-Quite-Contrary runs in and pokes them with spider-biters. I rend the velveteen to get out of this mess, run off with the big fat jelly lady in mad pursuit. Pursue me darling under your eyes. I love you by *mail* or anyway I can. Who, I say, *who* the hell are you talking to? Dialoguing myself into madness, MOON madness I've referred to before in this absolutely chaotic mundane drivel of a novel. Novel? *Whodunit.* Just answer that. I done it.

Coffee after we devoured the chicken. This chapter is about a chicken dinner with some new friends in New Mexico. In a big white adobe house in Placitas. People from big-city places. Matter of fact we can plaster each other's backs with mud we're so close already. I'm optimistic sitting here at home on my lonely stretch of the mountain, tip of the Sandias. Meaning watermelon. Lit up brilliant red in the sunset so often. Where the War Twins lived, but they weren't all bad of course. Brought the Zunis out of their last cave onto Earth-Land. My Gemini cohorts. A family of friends trying to make some sense out of each other's being a certain sign and other occult farts. Enough of that. This started out deadly serious, biting, asking for Death. After all, I got it in the future position in the Tarot the other day, wow. But today after offering some cornmeal, Quaker's cornmeal, to the six directions out at that great rock outside on the rocky cactus piñon knoll that's propped up on a small rock, and carrying out my Zuni fire kachina, I came back in, and the High Priestess showed up in the Tarot. Takes over Death's future position! But I'm still shaky. Isis she is, Popess, wow, at the door of the Temple, but this time feminine. All feminine.

Heinrich Schűtz. Concerti for 1 to 5 Voices with Continuo stemmed directly from the severe shortages and great hardship of the Thirty Years' War, 17th Century. The style "terse and the scale restricted," a pious supplication for a happy death and reunion with God. Gods.

Chicken and dog gods. Typical Christian ambiguity. I am the follower of your flesh. Following around talking about everything but. But. We fight under the curtain until we fall down all over each other. The fairy tale told. The chicken eaten. The messages garbled. The same record played over and over. Get together and make up our own music. New York's dead. San Francisco's dead. New Mexico's dead. Where it rises again. Poetry. Slap-diddle. Diddle-flap. ZINGDAP ZINGDONK. DONK WIPER. HONK WOMP. ZOOFLESH. VELVET TROUSERS. ARGUE ABOUT IT TILL YOU FALL ALL OVER EACH OTHER. MORE VIOLENCE. GET OUT OF THIS MESS. JUST GET IN YOUR SHIPS AND PULL OUT PULL OUT CRAZY MUD-FACE SAVING YANKEES.

The only hero is the guy who shows his ass. Join the jockeys stranger women. I'm optimistic. Here I am. Schűtz Schűtz *Ich hab mein Sach Gott heim gestellt.* Come to me, death. My favorite photo, New Mexico water running over the hands outstretched, palms up in the water. Come to me eating a chicken. New friends. Wow. We're open enough together. The community rests ZINGDAP on that. Death-love. Death-unknown. The dead chicken. Sacrifice happenstance. The mind stance pogo-sticks from one place to another. Do you follow? It doesn't matter.

Deep in the saddle we ride,
float out over the countryside.

High. Mind over matter. Through it fits, fits, sex-urge to friendship-lover. Ancient bud. Flower through the male. Ovary-suction. Sap-sap. Moment of recovery. Death cycle way down, lost. To zap back up. We *are.*

10
SUN IN WINTER

This nature of earth. Mother of nature. Mother of the earth. Rivers fall down upheaval. She waits in the anteroom while the dining room is destroyed. Earnest nitpicking. Twiddling thumbs. Sitting around while things outside crash down. Have already crashed down inside. Atoms balance atoms. Balance in the hands. Eruptions from them. Warmth is the healthy itch, burning is the damage. Cities on opposite planes crash into one another.

Prophets' written words rise up from books. Mouths take over, talk talk, running talk, shout. Watch, out there. State of the union, union is walking upside down, running, jagged, fall down, can't get up. Waterfall music. Violence goes through the spiritual machine. Blood runs through. We sit outside, smoke in the distance. Here on this hill mountains of music in upheaval. Strength, give me strength. Sea floors rise up, become fertile land. Waterfall of blood will be over? Friends leaving the country, buying boats and sailing off anywhere, away. Money falls into the right hands on occasion but the dope is fucked up. Contradictions, where do you stand? The oceans are moving. The poles charged up charged up, repeat what they've heard. It hits the Earth and the poles change. Mass rush, reversal magic.

Columbia the Gem of the Ocean
Turkey in the Straw
Old Black Joe
When I Survey the Wondrous Cross
Long, Long Ago

Quotes from quotes. Hearsay. Charles Ives' Symphony No. 2. Flying saucer music. There is a cloud behind the Sandias where the Mother Ship hides. They know. We've made ourselves quite evident spouting off above the atmosphere, violence down below. What are we doing fighting? The summer brings it, breaks it back in our faces. The power structure structured on the tits of the Mother of Earth. She wakes to the eternal tunes, far-reaches, music, waves of excited recovery. Come back, come back, I give you this drug. Medicine for the mind. To find, go through the body again back to the orientation of sage growing from the Earth. Rainbow domes. Skies alive in fright. monkey year, monkey year. Freight trains unhooked, barrel down the canyons. Mass murders, cities unlivable. Ives plays on from sea to shining teardrops.

Sun

is its own movement to finish the Piscean. Toward Reveille. Catastrophe in the basses. Judgment horns. The plenty spread around so people can use it, eat and live, hearing the old chants. The uprisen monarch gives up his crown. The new man walks toward it, takes it. The new man hands it to his friends. Put it aside and go out and build huts, dwellings – dig, plant, so, said before.

Sayings:

it is come
he is the risen serpent full of digital servants
the devil takes over when the going gets too rough
over the worst seas
landslides   thousands rush inland   pueblo walls bulge.

Atlantis in everyone's eyes. They all see it swimming before them they can't touch. Swimming to add on to the land, floats there. The man comes, leads us to it. Living through Genesis or what the electric mixer did to me when only the funnies in the paper make sense. It's winter now. The establishment ears crack open and split like sails on the Devil's ship. The Sun is fucked over, masses of smoke. Handmade tepees below, some of them already started. The first summer after the powerful Sacrament. The second summer fallen out of the books. Politics like mice scampering. Establishment with no pants on tries to run away. It isn't funnies funnies. Funnies. Funnies. Columbia the Gem of the Birdbrain. Birdbrain shits monkeys. Monkeys laugh and stick bananas up their ass. The mother of the mother, Grandmother of Images rises from beside the waterfall.

Sayings:

Children, the Savior is the RiverRun.
Ghost Tantras in the morning wave off flies.
Build. Move on. Move. Wherever you are working
be moving

(power plants zapped out by hovering saucers, the black men sick to death of being treated as America's lessers. Mass filching, rape, all colors, grab it he's not looking. More narcs more narcs that's what we need more narcs).

Mother, I love you. Mother of the Sun and the Father of the Twain, the Twins who led us from the seeping holes, the caverns of filth. The animals, our brothers. The new man is your lover and rides the high wave. Ellipses with no ending. The meeting of forces when good voices are needed. I am staying here through this. The test will draw me out.

The man in me starves "hysterically naked," shouts. Eyes *must* look into eyes. The third soul showers from the third eye. Libations poured. You can learn to do this too.

Volcanos, earthquakes, visions. At dawn. I am the sun. High to the point of walking, following the tide out to the new island. Wars against the orient. Mass hatred exposed. The Air Force finally leaks out the Flying Saucer men have us by the balls, shaking us up when we are still incapable of cosmic consciousness – the beginning and the end. Ellipses meet and yet we damage the gift and the new President's asshole is displayed in public. Assassination #2, 3, 4, 5? Quotes of quotes. The government is Mafia. Got people hooked on the devil – devils devil devils. Zen.

⁕

Buddhist chants go on. Hopi chants go on. Where are we in the filth. Twins, lead us out. New man, find us.

⁕

Water. Water pours through the constellations. The water-bearer lives by the waterfall, lives in the air, lives with the woman of Earth and all. To find him to be in us and her. To find him in us and all and her. Sun is the bodies of discovery. We are walking through the zodiac where the love lines cross. Gigantic parabolas meet in the source. And the rainbows of the source are in the source of the source.

Sayings:

I seek warmth
I simply seek warmth.

Having found it, rest in it. Or when cold move on. *Do something.* Give in to the given, the rainbow domes and the running river. Waterfall of the vertical paradise when men can't sleep and their eyes are propped open with wars. And the doors creak. And the winds tear down the houses, *mud.* When seas are calm and the people are led here is a beginning. Mixing mud, now frozen. It is winter and my mind goes far out through screens of words. The sounds of Ives on the phonograph, "Columbia the Gem." I look through, I take the gem. I swallow it to see you better. The ocean backs the tidal wave in my mind and lovers come and go. I will give you all of me in the working for the way. Stars in the Tarot, water in the Zodiac, friends around the fire. Love is through this, through us. The logs given themselves to burning in the mud fireplace. Warmth, draw us together when the spitting fires outside come near.

11
CONGRESSIONAL HEARING

The break. The thaw. The last snow. Voices from the next room. It's true, is it not, now you've come before the hearing. The demarcation line is noble. The winter is a face. Do you deny that or have your constituents a better solution? Anyone with a better plan should come out of his hole in the snow and erupt upon the face of the earth. Stress lines. We are the world of orange. You punch us on one side and we'll bulge all over. We've got to listen to our scientists. Fuck the intellectuals. Senator, watch your language over the air. Just stick to how we're going to withdraw our troops when the earth is shifting, the poles shifting, the rind of it torn and bleeding, no spirit left in the people. Squeeze functions have terminated. Face the panel and square yourself for the big news.

What do you mean, Mr. Secretary, I *am* the news. Do you wish to disturb the face of the earth with your bitter attacks? We're swimming in orange juice and you go around ordering malts. What have you, Sir. Check my record, Sir. I have, Mr. Weltschmerz. Have you any wool, Sir. Don't you think your hair is a little too long? This is television. Resort to reason when necessary, don't flounder around in the bushes. Madame, what are *you* doing on the scene? I'm Suzy CreamCheese the Miracle Maiden. Are you Exhibit A of false progress in the war? What do you mean "war," I simply give when I'm taken. Well watch yourself or you won't grow up like us. Sir, I've had my feet inspected and my hat's not on backwards. Just because you have no taste don't accuse others of eating oranges. *Only one question at a time please.* Should we sustain or call a smoke break. *You may not smoke in front of the explosives.*

Sir, my soup is sour. Do you expect me to eat this and talk at the same time? Of course not, this is an open hearing. Take your shoes off and illustrate your approach. Okay okay, that leaves me with one more thing to say. If you want to be peaceful, be peaceful. Mind your own nose and keep your fanny out of the pot. You see it's very simple. In fact there's no reason for this hearing. I've my nose and you yours. If that's really true then let's all go home for dinner. Well, I at least have previous commitments. Miss Cream Cheese and I were going to check on Mr. Muscle Man to see if he's still fighting the war. What war. I thought we got rid of that one. The war of the oranges? No, the one provoked by the naval treaty disaster. When they were sticking each other with bobby pins and calling each other names? Of course, dope. This is serious business.

We'll have to wait till the accounts of spring are all in. We've got to draw a line. Hand me red and green chalk. Spring will be unsettled. Earth will readjust itself. People will be taken by surprise. We'll have to give up our possessions. Just dig the grape juice, parden me, orange. *Lemon.* Muskmelon. Snake charmer, hors d'oeuvres. You *bitter comic*. Don't call me names. RAPSCALLION RASPUTIN RUMPELSTILTSKIN. I will protect my honor ONLY while taking a bath. Don't be coy with me, Senator. Okay, Shnook. WE WILL PROCEED WITH THE UTMOST REASON IN MIND. NOTHING ELSE. ONCE AND FOR ALL STICK THOSE OTHER THINGS IN THE CORNER. Have you got your cabin in the hills to move to when violence walks on the stage? Speak twice or forever try to stick your pieces together. I'm humpty-go-lucky. Have you any wool? Too much, black man.

She
was an ideal
woman
worth fighting for?
My appetite is green. Jump in the salad and prepare yourself to be eaten.
Before national television ?
Gentlemen, this is a SERIOUS MATTER.
But Mr. Senator-General, I've lost my composure. GET IT BACK. You lost your hair in the river. Get it back! Don't order me around. I'm from the South. Forsooth! Flourish! Madtime! PEOPLE EATERS. EGGPLANTS. ONIONS. BROKEN NECKS.

Ladies and gentlemen, the democratic process is at stake. I wondered when we were going to get around to eating. Soup, salad, and steak. That's an interesting American meal. YOU FORGOT POTATOES, EGGHEAD. Don't call me names, Tom Sawyer. The gentleman from Tasmania has the floor. Gentlemen, what I hand you is not on a golden platter.
You lost it in the exchange?
Please. They're marching on Washington. They're moving into the hills. They're turning into Indians and then turning back again. I've got one in the family! The family is defunct. Speak English please. THE OLD THINGS HAVE HAD IT. As they say down home in the corn district, Motha Nature is trying to get her house in order, stand on her own two feet, and doesn't give a fig for your reason. If that is so and I have every

reason to believe

POTHEAD!

it is, this meeting is adjourned. Thank you, Martha Washington, but we choose to keep on fighting.

12
ON THE MOUNTAIN

The world lost. A new land gained. Gains and losses in coins. Hills, flat land. A simple order of speech is an asset. Mark it blue. The sky the silver sat upon. A Genie without a master floats by. Come down. Bring me something I can't define. YOU, MASTER, CANNOT DEFINE. PUT YOUR HANDS ON MY SHOULDERS. I WILL CARRY YOU OVER. A simple command, stay in my hands awhile, carried on the strength of this mountain.

Everywhere I am is movement. The eyes rest on the corner of something and it is the corner of the world. I sail through the floating counter-balanced molecules and sail back out again in the flux of more. I want more all the time. The road in the moon. Up and down and then up more and down and then the downs are exalted over the downs there were before when you started out. I started out being spanked for spilling chocolate milk on the kitchen floor. I didn't do it. Or now what happened, you don't forget anything? Or do you forget it all. There are blanks that pulsate, plates of silver over the sky and I float on the giant's mountain shoulder. Each hair there a tree. The blank plates with no words written on them. The eternal memory.

The only limitation is the *threshold* to the world. As I am carried on the shoulders. The breathing mountain. The plates in the sky open up. Two great silvers carry moisture. The threshold to high is a diaphragm opening. Subtle closing. I read as it closes. What closes it? What brings the intermission time, down the hill. The giant is not a giant at all but is a mountain under me. And I am the giant/midget. No size, only proportion.

I walk out to see what the clouds say. They hang between me and the distant mountains, the signs between the Sandias and the Jemez. The cold looking down over the world into the layers of atoms, the delicate swiftness of the mystery where the fragile lies over the black of the ultimate. Illusion in fern folds, lace cells. Permissions of life feed through, hover, floating on the black lotus pool. Turn it over, follow it out, turn it over. Follow it out. Turn it over. Follow it out, go to sleep, the caverns of voices in these mountains. Turn the ferns and lotus blossoms over, and there are sunflowers with seeds you can eat. And Western Yarrow, ferny-leaved. A good smoke, and nearby.

I will carry I will carry nerve centers endless complexity. Turn it over and it is so simple. I carry on my own shoulders the mountain, the mystery. Rain is forecast. We pray for rain and then it is forecast. Follow out today. Disarray, intermission, to strike through. The lightning hits the tower. Illumination. When? Today is tapping on the shoulders, doing little things that, nevertheless, turn over, have the immensity of correspondence. When it all relates, there is no struggle. When there is no struggle, lightning strikes the tower. When we fall out of the tower we break through the shell, we sprout. The giant plants us, we, the giant. I am a mountain memory, the voices in the caves, sprouting seeds. Tablets in the sky with no mouths. Up down up down over. Over. Wider, wider until there is no threshold and I step out. The world is born every day.

end

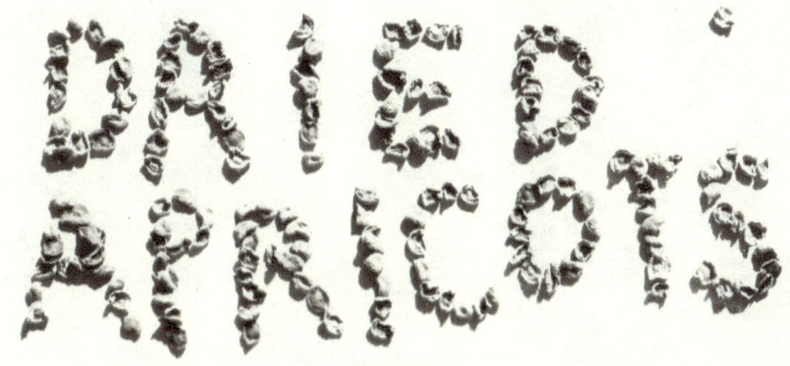

1 Maniac Dancer
2 Shame & Orgy
3 Male Longing & Secret Rites
4 Play Four
5 New Mexico Fruit
6 The Marriage of Friends
7 Freeman Songs

Dec74-Apr75

The door was open from the flagstone patio, the overhanging ailanthus trees and giant bug-ridden box elder. All was convenient only when the General and his wife were not in their big house. In our tiny adjoining free rent casita there were many who came in and out – Ann, Gino, Ken, Judy, Kell, Lora, Bob, Bobbie, Steve, Peaches, Mel, Bev, David, and many more.

1
THE MANIAC DANCER

for Ann (1936-1973)

it shall go on as
it goes on
go on in

GIFT : LENORE'S GARDEN

How often the gift to the giver is happenstance, or did someone else see the aura that followed flaming cool out from his head as he ran down the path to her garden. They met at the compost pit she dug so perfectly a meteorite might have fallen there.

So that God is within where I stand and her body under heaves opens and caresses out sewing machines into stalled cars, saucers hovering over Algodones power plant lit up at night, fire balls seen south, world turmoil in orison, a young man goes to the arms of his youth to the arms of his puberty, first union with her split like a branch from a tree. And therefrom hangs the fruit.

PROTESTANT SERMON: REMEMBERING THE PAST

Out of the darkness the coming is coming, out of the mouths of the false prophet Christs, out of the sour assholes of preachers and priests with their tired out songs and boring weight. The bands in sky open out wide fall as the realm of the other realm matches in donut shape the rising God offering love, no offering too often is an offering eaten in the back room by the solitary minister of malfunctions and hemorrhoidal pews. Aztec sky bands gathered like clouds overhead.

It was lost, his past, it cannot be told, it snowed, she went away, it bored him, the preacher got a raise as things got bad, he was merely writing and not listening, his son was eating pink grapefruit from Texas.

HE MEETS HER

And it came where he took it and it had no power but seen as a vivid scar in the afternoon when he sat clock ticking before the fire and realized the vacuum of the lost coming.

It was gained. It was inside, as hers is. It carried her with it, and carried him. He turned everything where it stood, the corn rows still talking in December wind, the broccoli growing six feet high, the garden waved slowly in the wind and stood over him as, upside down, he climbed in his coming to offer himself under her garden, on top of her absence, the real Western love he heard on the radio surrounding him and she called him, and he called her again.

SIR FRANCIS SCOTT STERNE

Fiction is the limitation of shared consciousness between two people. Yourself to a star, yourself to where you are, awash, speck, turmoil. She stood on the parapet and decided to fly away, but then she paused to write "The Star Spangled Tristram," and all the jokes attendant, but why, why did she bother? It can only be explained in a periodic sentence, so she struck out the Eighteenth Century and sat down with her quill in hand. A special pencil she shaved the paint off exposing the wood and put her name on it, Sir Francis Scott Sterne, eclectic mistress.

ANN

She went out to sea, to leave me. She walked into the water. She died. I get my mail to her back from England marked DECEASED. Ann. Ann. Time goes by, going. Goodbye.

A hurried note: only Mozart's piano concerto can be heard in times like these. A horde of deadly insects threatens the world. We are crazy apes. A mistress of nuts and bolts. A master of nuts. A hungry bolt. Sir Adrian Boult bolted out of bed and bolted the door. I was struck by a bolt of lightning. I was electrocuted when I waded out to try and save her.

MR. ME

An occult stranger of a cult ox. Stranger than fiction. Rubbed soothing oozing on the pre-Columbian fetish, little man sitting cross-legged, at last admitted into Godhood. It's been a long slow hard pull. Up. To get where the bannister is, and project yourself into God. God of the twain herself himself pardon me himself. Her self him self. Hers. His. Both hanging down. And then one hanging down. And then not hanging down. Nothing hanging down. The full swing into Godhead. God's head where the Christmas tree is. Lights blinking on and off. The whole thing sitting in a little bowl of water.

The tree. Piñon. The space moves me, into the crackpot of myself. The knowledge of where I am. Potted. Cracked. Pitted. Pacified.

ROUND EARTH

Christianity is the lug nut of the wrench of God, the God of old time passing. A lug nut has little depth for there is no need for it. Lug nuts hold the wheel on but everybody knows the little use for the wheel in ancient America. A golden toy perhaps. They had other uses for the round of the earth. The circular calendar stone doesn't need any nuts to hold it in place.

LOST NOVEL

We wrote to each other, dead. 39 horses lay strewn about, all the trappings of a mime in the park, white robes, Plantagenets, Elizabethans, masques *parfums*, exonerations, a return to an earlier century. It was all in her mind and wrote through him, she (Ann) had her will and he didn't fight while he was listening, but he knew he had to fight out of her character, out of her borrowed country and boat to the sea, the fantasies out-lived, the fairy tales covered with mold, the dead seagull she placed on the rocks washed back in when he took it out and threw it as far as he could into the ocean.

He was her left, and she was her right and she slept like a ghost between them and rose up cold like as they embraced. I turned to her and her face was ivory with eyes aglow, I touched her ivory arm, took every bit of strength in my body to kiss her slightly rouged ivory cheek. Cold. But that was that trip. Earlier a helping hand came out of the phonograph and I took it. She'd gestured it. And wind rushed through the doors and sunlight rustling the silver signs she called them. They were aluminum foil hangings. But she was on it, directly on it. She taught me how to arise, and be there, on it, at whatever speed or rather, standstill. We met best without ever moving, and that floated out of corpses burst open yawing messages she was always hearing, meanwhile, I am told, she was a sweaty fuck. Whatever modified her Godhead modified his.

MANIAC DANCER

He modified her Godhead and her bottomless God, by entrapping the tree inside her, and dancing upside down before her, a 12 year old English girl. He was the maniac of the dance floor, was moved by the spirit of the mountain. Do you remember when over that Thunderbird we danced, Martín Gurulé said, he was dressed up in 50's hat, and tie, and danced. We did these things where we got down on the floor, especially the Stones' eleven minute *Goin Home* that was centuries of Santa Fe gone down in decay, we avoided the capital city and stuck to the extremes of Placitas, Albuquerque, Taos, Mexico, and England. *Nueve.* Ann and I. We danced ourselves out.

FINDING YOURSELF

John, who shall we have over for Christmas dinner, a gay or black couple. John startled up from his bag of porno effects. Why not have a lesbian and a lukewarm vegetarian. He was always full of ideas that please. His eyes would narrow as he did the *bossa nova* around the room on the shag rug. This year it was Shag Purple. He collected popular ways out and had a carefully catalogued closet. He was the guy everyone wants to punch out in the novel, somehow he came through too clean. He always handed you a towel when you needed it most.

Character study, he said, passing the joint. I'm pregnant. Gloria felt like throwing up. She was with the wrong group in the wrong house, the wrong time the wrong city. Not only that she'd forgotten her G-string David made for her to protect her in all seasons.

John beamed. Would you like to look at Girdle's Stretch. He got up before an answer and popped into the closet. Everything began to collapse. The catalogs fell over and burst into flames. Gloria ran out of the house as the flames shot up. People were yelling. She rounded the corner and ran into the stop sign. The car pulled up and she got in panting. The guy was exposing himself. It was indeed him and it was indeed her.

BIRTH OF THE SUN

Superwoman directs. Go get a quart of broccoli from the freezer. And feed the rabbit and bring her warm water. Ok Ok. My ceiling suffers. My walls are sliding down, the floors sticky. We are moving slowly to another place. Super Pisces calls back from the ocean. I am the entire city of New York. You have disgraced me with your politics. Your red IBM typewriter.

Actually that was the raving old lady speaking, between raves. I have been demolished by popular vibes. There isn't anything pure any more, and yet need I say so. Your politics is always showing through those fart holes in your shorts. Your politics would straighten the Eiffel Tower. You mean turn it into a vibrating dowel.

Lenore is making a mask to scare people with. Isn't that a lovely thing to do for Christmas. Christmas, my Aunt's sack, you mean the Solstice, the birth of the sun. That is her mask. A big masculine American. You unzip the front of his face and out pops the beast he is. He's alright. I mean the beast. I mean the great big hunk of a man. I mean her. She means him.

I mean the birth of the sun. We are a long time coming when we come.

2
SHAME and ORGY

The vitality of God is in his Rod.
The Oval of Yore is in Her.

No offense is meant by the poet, only light reading for a cold empty night when your Newsweek didn't come. Or staring wildly at New Yorker there's a rampant urge to turn the page somewhere else in time. Italics mine.

1

Quick to grow up from the fire-rag wrapped around his dick, copal smoke billowed out in billows billowy bulls out into the room, for soon, and set the ladies all a-swoon. Heads with veils and ancient dresses floated on the floor and the first time son was held aloft by the macho Pisces father watery in time to snort his nose and bellow out, "A son is born and there's the yarn." The bar party drank the free pitchers of beer and out in a loose cold oval smoked the ship ashore. *My influence is my fear, and both contrariwise. The Poet spoke italics.*

When he reached the top he didn't stop but dreamed on through the night. He was there with Macho Pisces, Father of the Sun. He never gave me anything to look at but a dream, except a long time ago at another table in another bar he carried on his arms the hands of God, not the Sufi God he met behind the restaurant bar, but the hands of God dropped from the rugged Old Testament of faith between men scattered all across the Country of Supreme Space and dotted with the horny cavities of masculinity. Sooner or later all the sex of every man will come out dripping into the stove, to fire up to the God who made it dripping from his rod.

2

Meanwhile the curious sublunar ceremony carried on and his Pisces wife, daughter of the Moon and sacred Coatlicue Mother of us Aztecs without a rite, dreamed on into the night, and there was Prince Charming suddenly darker and handsomer. Oh if she only knew! She cohorted with him and searched to tell me of it when I saw her later in the dream night. I had him with me, did he look like this I said. This God here is the Plastic God. God of Plastics you did it with. What form he took to take her in, the old Hermes only knows. She'll have it anyway.

An old dead rotting cat on the terrace. Smells like cat shit. I dig. The lump recovers gets bigger rears up backwards, a horse rears back bursting back into the big house next door, recovers runs through rooms doors tramples turns over breaks everything in every room careens breaks all the windows jumps out and runs away. *The Mare.*

3

"Does God have sex or is Sex your god?" spoke the Mormon to his Mate. God is a momentary plaything, play while we can, "be fruitful and multiply." He drew X's and they fucked like dogs. Cross the prairies cross the mountains pushed his pregnant woman in the vale of 96 tears, mighty questions left to answer, find the pussy stick it in just like Joseph's disappearing chin. Smith Junior Cough! Hold your tongue and stick it out, fuck those holes in underwear, wear them under where she's bare. Have a vision when you're down and screw the whole town. Religion in religion out, nothing dear to shout about. Bring that old horse there to drink. "Shove 'em in by the head, pull 'em out by the tail." We live by the Golden Rail.

Climbing stalwartly to God he fell and broke his rod. Aaron's rod, God's rod, all the little creatures nod, our hero's fast asleep. Passed out, as his wife puts it, playing with his underwear.

4

Caught between the cold shoulders of his father and his brother, the Poet like no other is a mother. But he is not the hero of this bogus myth. Thith boguth peeth of thit. Our hero practiced fellatio on the navel and grew the hairs there we now see everywhere. His name like Randy Bulls pulls taffy over the eyes of die-hards. He's a Gemini, sometimes. Has sprouted wings on occasion, is slue footed, and handsome. Sooner or later the complete sexual history of every man will come out.

5

Sarah Bernhardt. And George Withering Spoon. Hold your son up to the sun and dance around. The fire sucks and pops and scares the dog. Everything is sacred if you place your place among the places. God shining with his hardon, seeks his careful union, has it had it shining knob on where he found her. Now she slithers everywhere up and down the bar walls, warm at home growing large, out pops the cookie ginger bread half eaten, baby growing nudging 6 days old and bolder.

When the West was won she won it. When day is done she done it. When the miners come she mines it. When the store is open she stores it. Freezer ice box Alaska Tucson San Francisco Mexico. Tough Nut Street. Women with balls are nine feet tall. Listen Nellie you're the Pisces woman won the West. Your doodads hung out outside the Catholic church and called them in. God's clothing hangs on the clothesline. God wears your brassiere and complicated undies no modern man remembers or has had to deal with. God is wearing long stockings, C-cups, God is wearing panties, garters, bustle. God is very old fashioned, strait-laced he comes out of his church to welcome the parishioners. The service will be ordinary except the priest will be in drag and very Nellie as he ought to be. He is the Priestess. At long last she is Priestess. Ordained and staid.

6

GOD IN DRAG IS NELLIE

I'm a priestess not a priest, says Nellie Carter, 28, one of the 12 women who defied the Pissed Couple Church last July by being ordained to the priestess-hood. "As Priestess I'm for mumbo jumbo and all sorts of pagan goings-on. Those who oppose us would love to call us priests."

Hermes young as old well we call him Herm the Worm, came up out of a hole in the Church the Sun son drilled when playing with his Christmas brace and bit. Herm the Worm Ginger Boy wonder of the chorus strong standing with his worm in gear singing Rock of Ages. He advanced during the Advanced Coupling Hour and when the offering plates were singing raised his robes beside the fire beside Nellie's altar. He caught her by surprise before she got her bustle strapped on. He flipped the Bible to the Song of Songs and took up Nellie on his Golden Church Rod, the Seamen Mass #1 Hermes Ginger bared her near the Altar, organ dishing oozing sounds Ravel and Pancake Man music as the plates flew like saucers pew to pew. The offertory struck gold, the Bride of Jesus sang her song Nellie Carter Ginger Boy, Worm in Gear the Altar Singing Pissed Couple Church, the lurch of Man and Woman Nellie Ginger pagan mumbo jumbo semen ooze and solid roof off service serves - Our Lady and Our Lord in Marriage Pancake Pagan Song. I love you and I love you long, the couple on the Altar. The Song on the Song.

I do not wish to offend you whether you are god or not or atheist or dried rot. Get up the horse and go. It came down where it stands and the Poetry of our Lord and Lady of Duality sits before the very same table that unearthed us altogether from the Loins of Her Lover and the Loins of Her.

7

WHAT IS REVEALED

It may be done with stuffed ritual objects. Large shadows of. Simple crude manifestations of the union. Complex hereditary commingling shapes. Or better yet, it may not be done at all. At home where you know it is going on below you or upstairs above you. Suddenly the pyramids are upside down and you are walking keys to the ever eye of the pyramid the top cones triangles noises the shadow of the words, the words singing round the corner when suddenly, always, something is about to be revealed.

And it was no matter what the struggle what the limitation of the salary the work conditions never get mentioned in the books, the books on the altar on the floor in the bookcase sing potential upward uncoiling backward plots uncircling gyrating still.

The oval mirror horizontal lowers to his knees. The Father of the Sun looks down and up. The ceiling is dark but reflects the sound. T-Rex. Gay rock. Spike Jones. Fats Waller. Ma Rainey. Disquisition X. The novel in jeopardy, continues as a force as you read your Sunday paper.

8

LIFE IS LOVE WHEN IT LETS US

And is a flying saucer. Somehow they got into the wrong room. They'd always suspected but never thought they'd meet there. There weren't too many years left and there they were. It was all written about. Suddenly everything fell together. He could participate in his mind and know it was time to let go. They were there and the wild pauses as people danced were even greater than talking.

The youth of men came directly from the Sun and smoked up from the stove into his muscles. One reflected the other's near craving desire. Suddenly barriers disappeared where walls were more secure. They leaned back and left to meet with the electric glow following as they followed where led and long talks till the last plunge met the blood drained out the doorways meeting. Life is love when it lets us.

The youth of women came directly from the Earth and grew up from the garden into her body. One tagged the other's near craving desire. Suddenly barriers disappeared where walls were more secure. They leaned back and left to meet with the electric glow following as they followed where led and long talks till the last plunge met the blood drained out the doorways meeting. Life is love when it lets us. *An object of the Fuck Divine.*

3
MALE LONGING and SECRET RITES
intended for men only

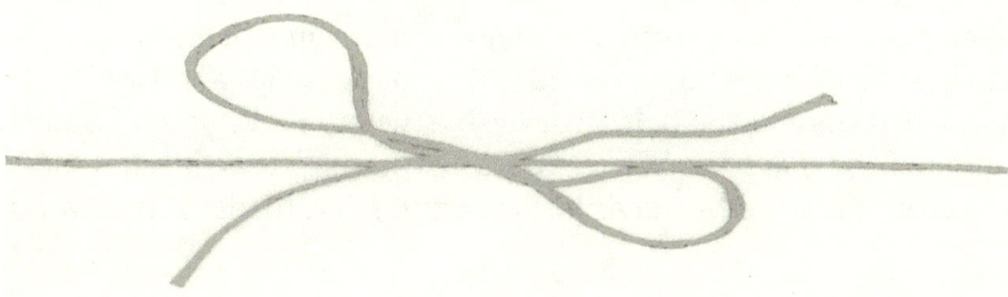

1
JOCK

Having been well oiled the beautiful former jock lay back on the waterbed the tip of his cock gracefully nudging the ceiling. She was up there, playfully, and wouldn't come down. What a tease. He nudged her endlessly, traveling up the shank of his cock, a tease, floating surf coming in the covers in a swirl around him. On his back, the slight beard, the Van Dyke, the muscles, the hair over his barrel chest expanding with his breathing as he traveled up and touched her lips with the back of his hand his finger entering her mouth she laughed, her hair falling down the sides of his cock. She spread out displayed on the ceiling, his head bulging with the news from the brain, the pot shots, the golden warmth, there was culture here surrounding, the swirl of colors of the bed around him, reaching up for her breasts hanging down, the tip of the barrel chested big man loud, gracing her cheek, playing over lips, the nose, every racket the Porno Poet knew, to treat him dearly, lower her familiar bush like a garden, into his retreat, beautiful full man lying back to her floating down closer and closer, the vision down the sides of his heavy light cock full swollen to delicate tender touch touch she touches down so beautiful her long light brown hair falling from her brown eyes slowly sinking into his arms. He is a lover.

She lies on him and he holds it deep sinks up in her wet enormous swallow, her bush cunt takes great gulps and holds, her lips across his cheeks and into his mouth on top of him, large former winner of the football hero's wreath, a University Star, holds her in his arms as she pops his cookie and he rises in her dreams as he sleeps, so lusciously.

2
THE GREAT WHEEL

"My sweetest Lesbia, though you are yoong I care not for these Ladies who cling to your tongue, for when we converse, her butt for a face, you speak through her asshole and despoil my lace." Sir John Suckling! at long last a member of the race? Which is exterior in absolute giant revolving form, the major disk turning of all time intermeshed with weavings of hand, Tibetan tapestries and Hopi designs, surrounding the belt, dear Lesbia, where I take you off and only the chink of the diaphanous undercurling rotating stone is left. Our history, ours. Dear Lesbia, dear John Suckling. Sir. Madam. Woman of Yore.

3
ESTHER THE QUEEN

It was so big they couldn't handle it. They rolled it into the town square and beheld themselves there. Who could equal it, not even the King, not to mention the Queen. She arrived in a flurry of haste with the entire bugle choir and trappings trailing behind, a hundred bakers, a hundred swimmers oiling their beautiful bodies the sleek America image everybody knows swimmers' bodies, a hundred cooks and a thousand soldiers of the Green Fork, where the River bends. She arrived loud and pompous, hands on giant hips and the Rubber Dick floated beside her on a pillow, so many servants the Sun did rise by itself, and the poor miserable King kowtowed behind her. There the Inflated Bliss, heavy in the shoulders stood, curving up from the Platform and throbbing in the sky, pearl dark, glowing, the Sun rising through the trees of the Exactly Spaced Park.

The Queen snatched the Rubber Dick from the pillow and strapped it to her mouth and blew. A flapping fart sound quietened the mob. Thousands looked as the bakers offered cakes around the base of the Giant Hardon. P-b-b-b! Hee haw. The donkeys stopped pulling as the bugles lifted to the lips. *Silencia* began. Carlos Gardel stepped on the stage, the Sun beamed down as the tangos began. The swimmers began the swim as the Orgone Fairy descended from her Statue and the Band played on. Esther was alive in knowing how she led. The Giant Hardon slid from its base and into the Central Pool between the rows of Gardens, the Fiddlers fiddling, the bugle choir swaying to Carlos the singer of the people. The Queen took her Rubber Dick off and raised her skirts, she moved to the music in the park, tango, as Esther and her swimmers swam smiling ruby-lipped in emerald Yesteryear, jets of flame building up between the synchronized arms legs of, adore, the cunts of Yester Yore, the head of the giant pearl-dark Prick splashed out of the Pools, head up, waving, throbbing to the filigree dance of the Orgone Fairy of its dreams, dancing out her veils, cast off around it.

Up giant from the lake the pyramidal head as the swimmers lay back, lapping water over hardons encountering the breasts. The Queen with her sacred bush waded in the water, stood on the boat as the oarsmen heaved, Carlos singing the sign of the people, hashish cakes passing from hand to hand, a hundred omelets at a time arriving from the cooks as the Queen, robes lifted, was rowed to the edifice, the Orgone Fairy dancing through the other dancers and circling through the soldiers of the Green Fork overhead, dancing down their pleasures, lost in the mazes of the Queen's formal garden.

She was rowed and her Bush touched the base of the pearl-dark cock, the cock of morn, the prick of the Tube-Sun, the giant waves of heat blowing down from the risen sun. She, Royal to the Tango of the dance, was lifted by the Oarsmen, haunches bejeweled, lifted to the crown of the gelatinous ooze overhead. She straddled like birds wings beat, hooked towed, plunged swallowed, the Queen lowering down as the Giant Prick subsumed her, she heard the voices carrying her tango to the Sun, the pools that fill the Earth, the rivers of cum. She sang "Orgone Fairy dance, dance me through," and her feet hit the water as the swimmers withdrew.

She floated on her back to the silence in the band, floated with the lightness of the hardon of God within her Godly Sanctum, erected in the labial lipped cave of the Gold Tunnel, Pearl-Dark Union, Floated with the Hard Giant in her, the Son of God in the Virgin-Mother, floated to the arms of the Swimmers of the Garden, lifted her back onto the Royal Dias where the fountains played and the Fireworks blew overhead into seed bursts, wind slightly lifting through the trees of the maze and hedges ending with couples at each end. The Queen succumbed and the Prick slid out, and back into the water, turning it purple. She rose from the dias through the banners and the bunting, into her royal chariot, where she looked out, coupled at once for all time to come, waving to the crowd and all kingdom come.

4
MALE

Just as I was admiring his tenderloins in the locker room. *Pbbbt!!* sorry I cut that one! Why do you fart? To keep us apart. What a beautiful body, descended of the gods, brought back to the locker room to step in the showers, look at how the buttocks trade emergencies for my heart, the slim line of hair between the stomach muscles rises to the fan out of strength muscle pectoral spread chest of the God's father in the competitive son and plunges into lower fan, bush that sprouts Poochy's large hanging cock and swell balls bag between the gorgeous trucker's thighs, look there and out it comes the honored stance between men. I fart because I care.

Just when you could dive in, just when you cared to touch, too close for comfort and I'll stay where I am. America Standard I *Pbbbt!* carry the flag pole and march to beat the band and fuck the General in the stand. The legacy of all the army's legs, the jock's spread crotch, the hanging understanding that keeps a man a man. A lowered cut to the right and belly grinding halt. I love to see your *Pbbt* because my *Pbbt* gets hard and wants to *Pbbt* you in the *Pbbt* you Gorgeous George perfumy star I'll *Pbbt* your *Pbbt* and fuck the *Pbbbt* it's exactly where you are.

5
MOLLY O'CONNELL

She was so big she couldn't get up from the chair but stayed there. Molly O'Connell I'll have to name your name. You wrote me a poem and framed it for my room. Molly you sat there and painted Mexicans with sombreros sleeping by the cactus, and sold them in Hinkles, sitting at a table, your huge fat rolled out of chairs onto the floor and bent at the ironing board and listened to your son play the Warsaw Concerto. You were everywhere and just across the street from me. Oh Main Street of course and you came to me sleeping by the climbing roses next to the Pecos Valley Coca-Cola Company. Oh Molly when I went to see you later in years, there you sat and didn't like it that I came when you were watching TV. Your favorite program I stepped on. So much for dreams now. They tore your little house down long after our house across the street disappeared. Large and fat. Large and fat. I love you like a little boy's dream.

6
MISTRESS/MASTER

Oh Morphidite God, I separate the stars, and pull one from another to be as you sit – man and woman, woman and man, any combination the senses within ritual, the coining of the day, the long lost steps to the fire in the dragon where the heavens turn around. Steps come back though worn and sunken step up to the abode where you lie. Transform yourselves in one another. Transfer yourselves in major head. I bow down and touch the ground, I love you in my head. I love you Fairy

Queen. I love you Messenger of Atman. I love you mistress of my dream. I love you master of my master. I love you Christ of my soul. I love you Ann of my world. I love you earth against heaven. I love you arms in my arms. Lenore of my dreams become dreams.

The dance. The round dance I enter as I have and have have have, I dance from the spirit of the mountain Sandias and Old Woman up there laughing all night. I love you with your beams like eyes of the world. We look at each other from twos and twos. Forever the truth as we meet here tonight. The dream floats down major faults that follow where the springs burst out and flow. Flow. Here in the dual operation of my heart, the kiva, the place, we meet informally, to read and look and take down the light that furrows furrows, waiting in the dark. The year starts out in the same old way. We walk down from a scarecrow with a giant prick in the garden on our way to unknown gardens, where, we plant our souls. Souls. Old word turned out of brothers of the sisters and sisters of the brothers of God, turned over, her charming ways. She speaks with true lips true through you, you, you. She speaks through you.

7
HAND TO HAND

The enduring imagination unreels the song. Only one woman here, dressed as a man, wearing the heavy brown eyebrows, hazel eyes, perfect teeth and wide lifting lips, ears with discrimination of all necessary wisdom, black hair there, Kali, Crone, Nymph, Virgin, Lovely Girl to Woman.

I accept in seeing the woman as man in the ring of us here, and every opposite mutually expressed, hauntingly, what man is not a woman disguised? She tries to kiss me, as I kiss ever back, my love, my wife only. We come together in January, time to start counting the Earth as a step ahead of us. Men talk and don't say any of this. My wife is in bed. We are getting ready to move. Men my men friends when will it be. When will the masters of us reveal themselves within us to free the change. A knocking on the borders of our bodies. Begin where we start, hand to hand, master to master following. All in a row the dance steps come from below.

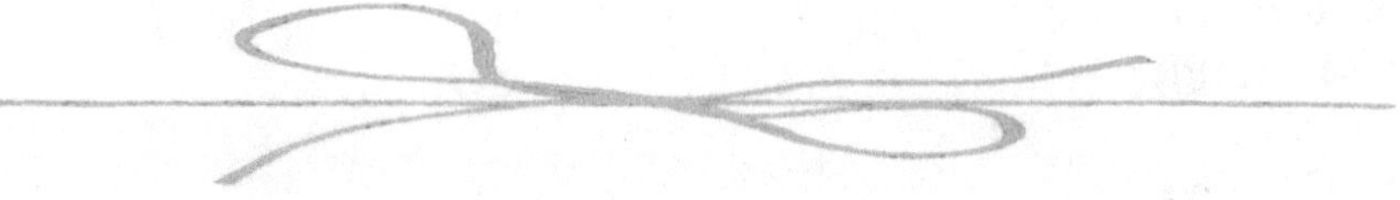

4
PLAY FOUR

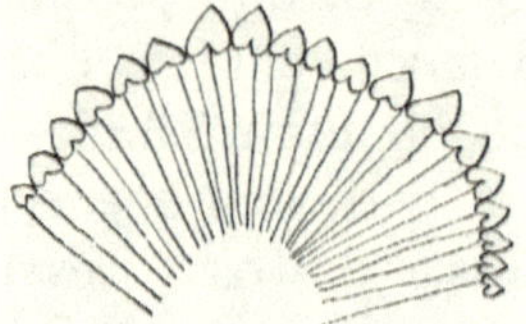

On this step in actual presence his head flared out in a half disk, like a picket fence wrapped around his head from ear to ear, not grinning, it all stuck out. There. It burst. It burst out of his head he was Aztec, better and closer still, he was Apache. His name began with 4 letters, a, a, a, a. The last the most difficult to complete, the 4th. The Fourth Symphony of Suck. Kind suck. You wouldn't do it if you weren't directed.

You are the Director. I am the Producer. I have vast wealth. Emeralds fall from my lips. Studded. I am the most powerful vision you have encountered, and there's no reason to think I am your last or your first. I stick out gloriously from your head. I complete the Fourth, only in 4 stanzas, in 4's, the Town Square, the major poet of our recent times said to me. He was my mentor and my head though we never saw eye to eye. He saw the humming refrigerator. He did not see primitive man. The cavities of his learning were so numerous he was layers of world mirrored broken in flux in contrasting and associated mirrors of the underworld. What was beautifully pitted like busted out bushes on top was immediately on the bottom upside down, the same landscape pitted piñon juniper washed out by Eastern ash sumac sycamore. Robert Creeley is my mentor.

Busted poked, sucked out of my head by my own reverse vacuum. Aztec dancers feathers splayed out from head, headdress seen in clarity poems seldom reach, ruled out by visual we can't talk. Stuck out suck flames, ears the bottom horizontal fan bottom, the headdress Montezuma gave the Old World a token of my referent.

❋

I produce this play which has the following characters.

ME with headdress.
YOU without.
MY MOTHER dead.
ANN dead.
MY SON alive.

MY WIFE alive and wearing grotesque fanged cloth mask. I have just taken a picture of her to verify this.
ROBERT CREELEY, who does not speak.
VARIOUS OTHERS who speak minimally.

✷

SON. All it is it's going to be a Circle, Mommy.

WIFE. You don't listen do you, I don't want you to do that.

ME. I'm pleasantly horny. If it were warmer I'd go out to the garden and bring in the digging stick.

YOU. An extraordinary woman characterizes the same old life you lead, you have nothing to teach and I'm only wanting something to learn. You don't read enough.

ME. I can't read when I'm staring at my eyeballs which have popped out of my head and are staring back at me.

MOTHER. Have you found your house yet, Larry. How can you live on what you make.

ANN. I come to visit you and sing over that knoll, Peyote Rock where we met the initiation of our Gods.

ROBERT CREELEY. Silent.

SON. It's just going to be a circle.

DEVIL. I have burst in to disturb the play.

WIFE. You are the nothing-most pigshit piece of scum that ever thought he was a dipshit in Paradise.

DEVIL. You Jews will have to pay.

WIFE. For what, Paradise? Better the heaven of Tlaloc where we bounce around.

ME. You are boring the Devil, Devil.

(Devil leaves.)

MOTHER. Take that off, Lenore, wouldn't you be more comfortable without it?

(She takes off fanged mask and sneezes.)

SON. It just got knocked over.

ME. My aura is not public, it is purely imaginary, it is the director's experiment in what is seen most clearly, the sex fantasies making love over the road as you drive, or the mechanics of space road windshield driving.

YOU. Ordinarily I might agree with you but you make me argumentative when you're so explicit.

MOTHER. Watch where you're going. Don't have fantasies when you drive.

ANN. Act out your fantasies.

YOU. You have come to a backward standstill, you can only go forward as directed.

SON. I got it rounder.

ME. Come back in yourself. The deliberations of vanity are killing me.

YOU. You.

MOTHER. I am your memory.

ANN. I no longer exist but my times will come, panting and coming times will come. Erect on the seashore, an advantage of myself. Skull and crossbones, a mask to carry. Everything is indefinite. There are no answers.

MOTHER. Don't rock the boat.

ME. No, Mother, we haven't found a place. We don't have enough room. We are actually being crowded out by our own art, and no room for others.

MOTHER. But your dad is giving you money to buy a place. And you'll have it. And you can visit me more often.

LARRY. That's true. As amazing as the vision of myself withdraws me into a cave, some hole someplace. But we've come out.

YOU. Shall I hide my tears or just go out in the lobby with them showing?

LARRY. I'm personal, hungry, always wanting a beer, entertaining but not popular, except around here.

YOU. There's only so much room on somebody's shelf.

WIFE. I'm sending my drawing of a living radish and the integral layers of other worlds and dried out mirrored reflection, the ghost-death of the radish – off to Washington D.C. to a show at the Smithsonian.

LARRY. If they don't accept it, it's another retreat to the hilltop. I guess hilltops are our caves.

ROBERT CREELEY. It's a muted landscape.

ANN. I can help you, Larry.

MOTHER. I can come to see you more often.

YOU. There may be something to consider, that's boring and yet not boring and yet bore-ass. Awful, I mean, now it's hideous.

(Wife puts mask back on.)

LARRY. The way she stands there as I photograph her. She won't take her hands out of her field jacket. I mean won't gesture or act out anything. Her long straggly hair hanging down from under the dark brown scale-petal mask hair. Her Levis. Her boots. My god how would you know she's a woman if I didn't know, except maybe the hips.

ROBERT CREELEY. Lenore, you're beautiful. *(Silent.)*

VOICE FROM ABOVE. Everybody knows that here, but there which is also everywhere, I'm the director also.

LARRY. You're the whitewashed evil elephant of an angel.

(Voice from Above falls down in the middle of everybody like a cloud of white flour.)

ROBERT CREELEY. So much for God.

WIFE. Who cares what we're doing when it's an extension of a personal vision.

LARRY. I know they don't but you've got to lead them by the hand and say, "Now art-goer, take your milk toast and when your stomach is settled, look at Lenore's drawing."

YOU. I'd rather not. I'm into crafts, stained glass macrame and spaghetti murals with health food on the side.

MOTHER. I died right after President Kennedy was shot, Larry, remember that, I want you to have friends and make it as a poet. I want you and Lenore to be happy.

ROBERT DUNCAN. Some poets say other poets are not poets.

ED DORN. My River is not changing its course.

ROBERT KELLY. So much is to be said, it goes without saying.

ROBERT CREELEY. Silence is a fucked up situation.

ERICA JONG. You're not in except as a creeping minority.

DAVID O. SELZNICK. Stare at my mouth.

DAVID BENEDITTI. Spaghetti murals are a touching interlude in the Post-Nixonian decline.

GLORIA. You see, Jewish rituals have more meaning than the meaning of the kindest Golem. Goyim. Go down Moses. Suck my God.

ROBERT DUNCAN. Carol Bergé unfortunately could not grace us with her presence.

CAROL. I had a delicious nap at your house, Larry.

ROBERT BLY. I left my shirt at your place, Larry: And also had a good nap on that incredible ornate bed some itinerant painter painted.

ANSELM HOLLO. I left my black turtle neck shirt at your place, Larry, and had one of the worst trips there. I thought I was going to die, I did. Arlene Ladden pulled me through.

CHARLES OLSON. Between me and Jung there's geography.

FEE DAWSON. I'm glad you're doing it, but you never did it.

GARY SNYDER. Yeah, I'd like to see where Larry Goodell lives although his "Ode: Thoughts Have Wings" is overblown.

LARRY. Where can we find a house. What spirits there are here, are as docile as spirits are. The wild drunks here are the spirits. Where are they.

TERRY. At the bottom of a bottle someplace.

STEVE. You got it where you want it. Your friends and my friends.

What more do you want.

BERRY. How often do you listen to what a woman says, and says it so completely it shuts out any man who is there.

YOU. You see?

ME. I listen to my wife.

WIFE. The act of work in a garden, the garden, the garden where the voices you hear and those things that sprout out live from your head, any time of day, is a slow simple message. Have you read *Islandia?*

BILL. It's as ordinary as the time of day, that's when I stay away.

LARRY. Different persuasions all the time, we rub up against and decline.

YOU. Except you're going up and no longer will be the figurehead of Placitas.

JOANNE KYGER. I'd like to see your act.

LARRY. And me yours.

YOU. Who has acts and who is just a visual poet, and who really rubs up against the trees.

DRUM. Did you say steers?

MARTHA RAY. You like my mouth, take it while I lean back displaying my tits on the back of the grand piano.

KEN IRBY. A collection of stars.

JONATHAN WILLIAMS. A collection of collections.

LARRY. To dance in the morning with some pink on, to the East and around clockwise. Four of us seems essential, two men and two women, we dance East, South, West, North 2 times, the four of us seems essential. And in the afternoon we wear some blue and dance East, North, West, South, counterclockwise, a couple times. And so, I say the old doctrines pay. She doesn't wear a mask every day. I don't get drunk every day. I don't want to be at the other end of the vodka bottle.

But
I'd like to carry these boxes of props in my Datsun to any of your way, I mean, to set up what I have to say.

Or
this is text of the Sun gone mad, no, we look for his house. There is nothing here to say. Said. Particles exploding from my head. Tubes, feathers, lines shooting out from my head. What am I to do dead friends, my long lost acquaintances? My lovers. The checkers on the board.

SON. Now I use purple on it. There are two ways.

(Wife doing the crossword puzzle.)

ME. Everything is broadcasting out, tonight.

WIFE. Stop it. Stop it!

5
NEW MEXICO FRUIT

"the nymphs and native Godheads yet unknown"
John Dryden
Juicy Fruit is the found poem of the godhead.

1
IN MEMORY OF BARRY JENKINS

We will waltz around the Cubicle of Paradise, our turbans with an emerald and a feather on it. You look in the emerald, it flattens out into a sea of mottled jade-like, a green and white sky. I look into the mirror of jade-like and see his eyes are below. He has a goatee, his arms are crossed. We are magicians.

Oh Barry and your Harem, part-time working Girls, but really Barry they are high school friends, guys dressed up in veils and dresses dancing around you in one, one of our high school extravaganzas. Barry you got hooked on drugs and went down to Mexico and died there. The Magician opens out his mirror in the hand of his head. We knew nothing then, and little now but the picture in the mirror of crazy jade. It envelops and stretches out, Barry and his Harem dancing between us.

2
AN END TO GERTRUDE STEIN?

So after middling and meddling in middling, Middling America meddling in a muddle, a muddle of middling muddling, we ended it all and having ended it again and again we blew it up, having middled it we muddled it and that was the end. To come out of it again having no beginning just to muddle it up again, having ended it.

I am talking about the short end of your digging stick. It is sticking out from her. Where She walks, it walks. I am talking about Spider Woman with a hardon going out to sting her fly. What can he do there struggling. He dies, to be eaten. I kill Her and sweep the cobwebs from my door. Oh I sing, I sing here weaving, she comes to me with her beautiful hair and large hips. Re-spinning, re-spinning. Ciel in Guatemala, my weaver friend, comes to me turning spinning, singing as I spin a yarn.

3
POET ON DISPLAY

This is prose heaped in rows called sentences, to talk, talking out to get out answers where we sit down, talk. We talk. Listen, I write more than I read but read a lot in little snippets, maybe someday I'll finish a book. I keep finishing them and finish them, fill them to finish them. Why start another book, why run out of space on the shelf. Build some more, sooner or later you'll have the entire Castle to yourself. Where her thighs are. She comes to me singing you're a clown, no more. Only a clown. Why does everyone laugh, they don't. Shake your skeleton. Come out of the closet with records falling on your head, art objects.

You are an art object. You ought to be demonstrated in some museum, on tour. This is the Larry button, he will now press it himself. Open the cabinet but don't stick your hand in. He has been known to bite museum-goers.

He dances before her angry mouth. He is trying to appease her, please her, she's a wild-eyed mad shrew termagant screaming fanatic woman. Her mouth is open, fangs, he dances closer. She sticks her tongue out, trips him dancing, he falls in, she swallows him up. She has eaten him and that's that.

4
MIN

What I'm going to teach you is the Exposition of Character. Delineate your ancient Egyptian prick God. Min. He turned to his Encyclopedia of Gods. There above the table on the table around the table is Min. Jacking off.

Follow along the lines of the Chart of the Gods, Table X hits the Spot. Earlier doshes and dats. Dat dosh Gods. Gods that spin out character, character of moldy souls, molded character of souls. But Min comes to life. One hand low, one hand high, ancient jack off god. The penis of his statues at the entrance of temples is well touched, springing to the defense of all fertility.

Eat plenty of lettuce, plenty of lettuce, it will invigorate the soil and the male. Pharaoh must ejaculate to be a good Pharaoh, to be fit for the ancient murmurings amongst the gods, I mean you and me. Moom mean meanie! No matter what you do you won't forget. Ancient history. My hand is up my hand is down leafy leafy lettuce. Flail away and grab. I'm holding my own, are you?

5
THE DOG BROTHERS!

The Brothers. The Dog Brothers, the World's Oldest Rock Group. We Rock together Boys because we're Colorado's own. Ancient rock orgy brothers hale away from home. Rock early and rock long take your pumas into song. You outlandish tall honkies with your heads out in the stars. *Vers Libre.* We go together poets and authors though we never meet. Musicians and concubines, whirling dervish clubs, oriental splendor of Arabian Nights with Tasha, Mistress of the Club.

"Listen Boys here's your delineation character. My separations are the intense plunge divides between my legs and shoulders. I breathe and I'm a walking PA. I announce all the energies before they happen. I'm a little like the Sun before dawn. Tasha the Divine Center for Rolling Your Own. You guys like to dance huh, well let's drop the lettuce and hold up our defenses and congratulate our horny selves. With the Dog Brothers who love poets and the dance masters of the present union are poets, dusty poets that nobody wants because they are the epitome of poets. I am a poet and I'm beautiful because I'm a woman poet, I am the minority of the future, pleasantly based and with a thrill on top. Don't flatter yourself. I'm not talking to you, I'm not talking.

"Here's the band, okay boys and my God a Dog Sister who used to play Bach. She still does. But with the curious distortions that our breasts allow us. So that the rays of the Sun are refracted back to their source and the distortion is prior to distortion. An obelisk is a petrified ray of sun. Light. We dance where we previously erased our existence. We no longer do anything but move with the crowd. I am the crowd. Falling down in double lines the dancer and the danced, the bodies you freaked out got ahold of bodies singing slinging. We dance to Dog Brothers, Sisters Mothers. Fathers and Gardens of the lovely love letter. Colorado New Mexico, I pronounce you Man and Wife."

-Tasha

6
MOON CALL

There is no mystery, which is the haunting secret. Stacked singing voices, tier to the Moon. The wind moves me up singing with them, all the way. Having erected myself in her chambers the curtains fall on all sides, silk let loose, falls, floats as my hardon snakelike head rises through and onto them. In her white bed.

7
OLD MAN

Septuagenary. Old man I meet in every direction but backwards, sing us the old songs again, and blast the aspen paintings off the shores of those northern lakes we hiked up to. Old Man of Old Men enough of this gossip about the Muse, this horseshit most poets vomit. You are the Grandfather blood and bones in my lines, I channel everything to you and get it back in fingered form, it comes like that handshake in the bar where we met first face to face and could talk unlike my grandfather, as he's silent when I ask for old tales, you're forever chasing one and told me time again to sit down by that tree and listen. So I yearn for your company most in the winter when it's so cold I can't see you though I know you're at your best.

We've been talking here a long time, a long line, and so it goes, January almost empty the weather pouring out, I'll up to see you tonight if you're healthy and well and can tell me what you told me the other night, "Yeah She's a good lay but a hard one and she cares for you, just don't lose your marbles in that bed, or you won't have anything to tell anybody when you get old."

8
THE FLOOD OF POETRY

Which is all made up, let flow, don't know, how. But meant if any flow-thing is meant to come into your kitchen or boudoir, my love, like an early note to spring, to open a book and actually read of the peace let down here to rest on the violent waves that gave birth to it, it rains.

People work too much on their poems. It is a thing not to be believed, the hours it takes, but washed out with the flood. The flood I wait for is all the garbage writers who fill up history with a mighty H and fill our mouths with deflating footballs. Wash them all out. Fouls Barf Pupdike Smeller and Epsom Salts and Gangarene Hernia of the academic vibe, the poets who devour pens and paper with revisions and have revised their own souls out. Washed out in the flood like a second bull dyke, the mother of the gay god that never got born, and formed a legend about the putrefying saints. They've all gone out shopping too late, the stores are closed and they're writing on the walls. It'll all wash clean some day, they tell me, little knowing that they stink from their own deaths.

9
READING ALOUD TO THE MUSE

No one knows if his poems are any good because he reads so well, no one can tell. Which face has the Tony, which the vacuum, which one roars after dark and shakes the bed? Why don't you tell me and tell me do. Why are you silent when I read so well, why did you laugh, why are you laughing, why did you destroy everything in your closet and come to hear me read in the nude.

Sorry, I'm the one who's exposing himself, over and over it's all in the game, nobody can ever tell.

What will she do next. Next she does it. You never thought ____. Blank, she fills it and extends the room with herself. She shakes the rain, rips the corner off the door, she steps in whenever I recognize she's there. It's only a memory of someone dead, she only comes in over your head, she only laughs over your shoulder and dances with you there. She enters the second part to announce the third, Mistress and Empress of the Empyrean when she's on, she's on. The Devil may care. When we come out together, our Force in arms, there won't be anybody there.

10
TEN O'CLOCK

"Humility" said the clock staring me down. I let the beautiful old oak clock run down.

At the top of the run you will hit the ceiling, come down with the dizzying turn of the earth you don't even see when you see. Awake when you're asleep, knowing you've got to work for a living. You get up and hope your house won't burn down, while you're up on the ceiling.

11
SUSSISTANAKO

Floating mysteriously with his ear to the ceiling he heard the bumping of God, like chairs dragging, and the chandelier with Czechoslovakian crystals he cleaned every month started swaying. He inched along but his leg drooped down and he started like peeling off the ceiling floating down just as he heard a clicking and high voice like a child playing.

Do words have any power? A power do, like a hairdo at the end of a finger – a worm getting a permanent.

Rays flunk out, bands disappear around the head. I'm obviously the Virgin Mary traveling backwards until I'm in the arms of Jesus and can't speak a word. Erase your indulgences and keep the worst thing you can say. Words have power. Decrease your vocabulary. Go backwards in time. Change your sex for a fresh breath of air and give a certain friend a break. A friend in need is a friend indeed. Amen, Sussistanako.

Old Goddesses are no more moldy than their worn out Gods. Speak to them as your ear travels along the road. Go back to cotton in a bowl. Go back the only way we can. His power center rests in the bowl she carries. Cotton, bumpy seeds in it, in the mica earth bowl I got from Ann. But when you breathe in the seeds they'll stop up your nose. So don't. Sussistanako will help you.

Burn copal in the Ashley stove, open it up. It comes out, it goes up out of the bowl bed where I walk on coals in bed, up the shiny tower through the ceiling through the hole there and out and up and through the clouds that hanging over brought the rain and washed away a lot of old snow – through them and the fog against this mountain, I'm leaving with the smoke up and through it all and up in air, face the sun again.

12
THE USE OF MESSAGES

To turn around in exact place where you stand, so that you face yourself turning to the right as you stand, peel off from yourself and leave yourself behind. Walk to the crevice out from the hill where a spring used to be, there find the buried mirror Indians buried to stop the spring, destroy the mirror and put up there your willow sticks and feathers, dampening the crevice with your spit, kneeling, your body comes back into yourself as the water flows out and the Spring flows again.

You can't allow that to happen unless you give yourself time. You announce the miracle and the Christians shoot it down. You allow more time to fall. But on the horizontal you settle in. My land. A strip of fertile totally usable land. You wake up the village with your moving in. Plenty of spaces in time so that you won't have to eat your words. Miracles are like bells strapped to the body. They work here in New Mexico but remember your Mother. Old Mexico. Remember your Mother Arizona New Mexico. Remember your Mother further North West. And further North West. Remember the bears, the northern bears, when the lights all colors descended hanging curtains dropped into your eyes. My father comes from the East, remember your father. North East. The European host. Like a disease my father's father's fathers spread into the West to meet her coming down and they settled here, worked out their cures and raised a child.

Those who wake hear the words passed around. It didn't take that many just to drive through the town and see it settling in the way the light came down from Northern skies into my wife's eyes. We live the former times inside us opening back the veils ripping the Priestess' sanctimonious curtain from her.

To actually build up from the ground as if I had no beginning here before, the muddled ending ended where we actually do set down right where I've always thought I was already, I wasn't there yet, in the village, in the pleasure of her heart when the curtains flow back. Fallopian tunnels breathe when she holds up the red bandana and it breathes in her hands. Air inside hands reaching through the circle of the necklace, little clay spirals strung together, he reaches through and it doesn't break. It is exactly as it was before.

13
BUST OUT IN SONG!

14
THE YOUNG MAN

I sing to the youth in your body, Our Virgin of Guadalupe didn't have any greater auras, zigzag green light outlines your body. My God you look like Billy the Kid. Cowboy hippie come a long way, you're the victim up to a certain pressure, and then you turn the tables and get out. I combine you two so your auras blend into the magnificent youth as you stand. "I sing the body electric" the Poet said, of you, young and the host to dreams where I write you out in worlds we combine our spirits in, the world of dreams adds sustenance to our lives here as there, the aura wraps around you, saw-toothed glow floats you up the road where you hitched here to sing out through your skin into the giant poet's mouth. Body into song line into juice below the mountain, fruit trees bloom, let fall frozen fruit now, sinks into the young man's dream. Around the edges of the village we make our yearly swing around to circle in like the aura's zigzag flow. Your body is hers. And hers is the lay of your body next to hers. The way it lies out. Recovering all the end pieces of the stopped flow. To bust out in song. In February strong as right and wrong. Sing what we may.

15
MY WIFE

Dipping down down in her for her wealth and riches, in store, laying there, she gives you everything and her young man-in-attendant's only there as a guise to turn the other women's eyes. I reach through the dream through the young man's exterior through the masculine surrounding like a fortress round a body, reach through and find you warm to my pleasure. Husband to Wife. Reach and hold you warm in my bed. We enter instead. We hold each other with the guard on guard. It is ours here and the turning sun spins out somewhere the other side. We'll see you in the morning. Her hair is in my hair. The hair burst out from our heads into visions. Living here is the preparation of our needs. We walk and descend from the mountain and its noises, into the unknown, known together. The family of a woman is the key to Paradise.

drawing with sky band by Lenore Goodell

6
THE MARRIAGE OF FRIENDS

1
THE COLUMN OF LIGHT

The Voice darker, got down lower than the feet, gravelly, pushed me up, carried me up to the ceiling where I held on, pictures broken images, me down down to the bed I bounced up from. And sat there. Just a joust. He picked me up by the calves, I stood there, lifted me, caught me when I fell down far below his feet. He dropped me down there and left me.

I got up and walked on down to the water still running in the arroyo. I saw him laughing beyond the bend and walked there not afraid. That is where we met. This is what we did. We both took a drink and sat there. There wasn't anybody else, it separated out of my body and sang there standing like a pure light with dark lines around it, out, from its tall white center, the column danced and bent right where thoughts popped out of our heads and met there dancing and bending. It floated between us sitting, slowly beyond the water, over it broke on off, away. Water in the *acequia madre*, sings up between us glistens over our bodies, glistens over our eyes, meets in the light that dances us out, the marriage of water and light, the friendship of our sight.

2
THE TONGUE IN OUR LINES OF SIGHT

It met, 4 lines meeting 2 by 2 focused on the tongue. The tongue licked up out of the dirt and stood out there. Our lines of sight focus on it wagging slowly. Wagging. I won't fall in, be tripped in this time as the mouth pushes back the dirt and opens there, the tongue sticking up. We sit there watching but it is more than looking at, it is being what it is having been with one another long enough to sit this way, watching out the tongue now the mouth. Dance. And so I get up dancing, hands clapping 2/4 to the 3/4 of my feet, standing run in a slow turn counter-clockwise. My friend simply sitting as if to guard the tongue with his eyes hardly moving from it as I dance clapping in a turn to my left like the rising morning glory turning upwards, the tongue still there withdraws into the lips, sand around the lips opening shutting I sit down panting. *"Stop."* I breathe. Our eyes focus on, *"Say."* I say. *"Say what I say."* I say what you say. *"Say it together what I say."* Say it together what I say. *"And say."* And say. "And said." And said. The tongue, clicking, stuck out again, the lips disappearing in the pushed back dirt. The tongue licking as if its hole should be licked, disappears, back in. We look, pat the top of the slight hill where it was. Look at each other, and go.

3
THE MORAL OF THE TAIL

The Power Goeth On. And therefrom hangs, the moral to the tale. I listen to you Completely. Completely I do.

The Moral? Be moral. The Tail? Be tail. Let them seek tail, and be tail. A tale to be told. I told it, and lived to tell the story. There is the other Story. The story of the Dead One. The one who stayed dead. They didn't have any trouble with him. He is your brother, your lovely Mobius Strip. Your brother is a mobius strip. You get cut apart but then you hang together. You are both alive, or both dead. You are never half alive, and half dead. One and two makes two. Obviously. Until the end. Two.

4
JANE RUSSELL, MY WIFE

She called because I was not looking at her and her voice would not be outdone. Femme greed. Power grid. I see her working out in front of the Olympic team, they are dumbfounded and sit back in gorgeous display of their perfect muscled selves, passive, passive, before her beautiful upright voluptuousness. All is sex! And the passage in and out where the voice of her clear calls call, animal looking down at the sportsmen putting notches on their guns. "How many have you got and what color." Oh she says Chicanos and Indians are all equality to me, barracks talk is barracks talk. "I wouldn't kick her out of bed," the soldier said. White trash or red trash it's all the same and you're to blame. "My old lady," you say, you said. The shoulder of her hip glimmered under the sequins of her dress dancing with Marilyn in *Gentlemen Prefer Blonds.* The mountain shoulder came down in a spring, through the rocks of the road and there's a picture there! The slow dance in the memory of split heads the morning after.

Oh Jane

Oh Marilyn, not to be outdone, you wiped out the Olympic team and glimmered through your mouths, into my ear. My ears aren't ears aren't anything near. But seeing flying like the bird I am, out the window where the black and blond haired women rake the old corn stalks and horse high broccoli aside, I see you through the window which is key to my soul when hands clap and the opposite panels interjoin and the dance you thought was dead starts humbly up again.

She sweeps   rakes   pulls   out,   cleans up the garden as her hair falls straight down where the men are sitting, beautiful no less. They, part of your life and mine, the other part.

How many times a day must I say that we're a part of each other, and the hundred headed things you and I do are for *ourselves* as much as each other. To say what the *doing* said is too much to say, when, you Jane Marilyn come at me on all fours, hip a mountain where I've lived and will live at the base, we slope down together in the eye for each of you focusing, folk us seen. Seen us today without anything to say, is the silence given over, shared and spread. The bed has a clean green sheet on, and yellow stripe with flowers on, in the living room. Come equal *equality* where no rude thing is said, really, drunk or far away, both ends meet, to leave, and say. An eye for each woman is an eye, to meet, broadcast it out from the garden   bed.

5
COURSED ADOBE

Mess grates the soul and builds up the altar of the walls in old coursed adobes. There are no bricks but layings of layers right up from the pit, of refuse and mud, wait a couple days to dry in the sun, and build up the next layer, a foot or so at a time, like they did at the Scalp House and Castillo Viejo, at Picuris. 9 stories, 80 feet high. Human scalps hang taken down only for ceremonies.

6
THE DEAD, GOD

To speak plainly is to say whatever is said, has been said, by the dead. To be one of them is hard to say, plainly, what they say. Why open your mouth if you don't dream. The pencil inside your dream is showing. The pencil I write with is showing. Through me, like water. Through it, like lead, on the page. A moving lēad. *To* something. Some sunshine. A poem for Kell who will be there. To Steve from Steve. To Minnie from Ha Ha. Not very nice. The dead to return and live crashing singing through their teeth they must have. Open the bottle, pour it out, the wishes and dreams. The pencil moving dishing out, dead pan out of dreams. Dead pan alley. Did pan out. Into the Fire. The Fire I worship, in the stove. Copal on the hot coals, frankincense, up the air to him, Man God, Alive God, Sun God above the hailstones above the clouds, a Mind God with a great big eye God, Triangle Eye God in the

Middle Eye God, too *big* to pry God with his feeling eye God, I see or Die God, what's in my hand God, or is it odd God, that I dig your bod God. All day long God, I hold your dong God, in the big fat cloud you stick it down give me a hand and lift me up put me to work and set me down, a work and play God, to be on the ground God, and rub around her big fat toes her belly knows the feel of his knob God, from heel to toes he gets around, and spends all day down on her floor God, with his big fat rod stuck in her Bod. I dig your God Bod, she's all for sure, she sleeps down here, we come every year and see what's up, don't interrupt, a simple care, we're everywhere, where you are now, Bod, I call your game God, which has a goal, bowl, like a greasy pole bowl, I love you both God and reach the Goal. Bowl. Your sacred wish. Your sacred come. Her sacred flesh. Her will be done.

7
KEEPING THE HARMONIES 12 YEARS

Twelve times I have started the water flowing, in the Springtime, around this pool. By being here am I a resurrection of the spirits of this place, dancing. No. Just a passerby, on the fly.

7
FREEMAN SONGS

1
THE KISS

Boring a hole into God, I felt his penis sliding in the hall, along the walls like neon lights at Irma's, and up my pants leg like so many ants, I threw off my pants and leaned over the immense globular flesh of the holy spirit. God, I said, what sex are you, cause I can never see all of you. He replied *I am a Man*, the Voice came tumbling over the massive ridges of loose skin of his rod, begging to be sucked and caressed. But I was too small. The walls of the cathedral were shapes of thighs, the legs of trees in the forest where I walked through the mirror and kissed him squarely on the mouth. As a matter of form he spat to the side *Ughghgh*! But he didn't hit me. Having advanced too far on Wild Turkey I backed off as the women stared, disgusted. The absolute grace of the incident escaped everyone but the teller, as I finger the story-teller's string with hidden images tied to it, reminders along the way. *I am a Man* he said voice rolling down the wrinkles and veins of his swollen prick as I kissed him squarely sexily on the sex organ of his mouth.

2
SONG FOR US WHO COME TOGETHER

Sing I sing I sing I sing whether low voice or high as apple rings. Sing I sing I sing, coming everywhere if you're crazy if you're spooked coming anyway carefully we come, a gift of everywhere for the naked Buddha who needs advanced care. He puts it on and hides it and offers us a fig, a seed for each man, a tree from limb to limb. We grow *into* each other walking in the circle, Buddha or the King naked in the middle, given up the gift, the hunting and the Queen asks what we're doing, we don't mean to be mean. We're simply holding hands, advancing in the dream. It's darn near as funny as anything you've seen, this dance we do together Grandmother hasn't seen. She's dancing in heaven, a hard worker's dream, we saw it in ourselves, the man in the Center, we behind the sky coming into us out of each other here in the middle, one for each of us turning in the center back to our homes, fortunate to have, here in our hearts, woman in our hearts, chest to bare breasts, alive to the hilt, softening the sword, hardening the plough. Turn her tongue under, seeds of her eyes, toes of pearl mornings, the desert in her eyes, dew across the brow. She sinks into our bed and rises with the thrust, infinity's dust. Hold our hands till morning when our children wake and our friends work away but come over late. Picnics and feasts sacrifice suffice, water in the morning, food late at night.

3
SPRING DITCH CLEANING

Bounty in the beauty full
walk on the hill down
in to the Village Pla-
citas Spring.

Song for every other brother
every other sister,
cleaning out the spring,
cleaning up the ditch,
that's what it means.

end

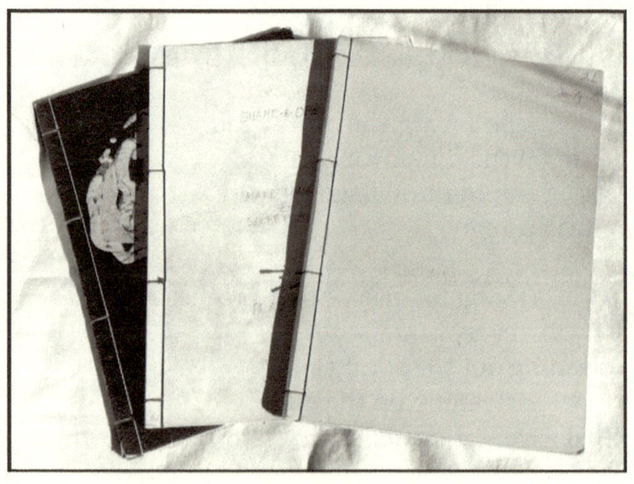

"You don't mention apricots once . . . ."
Stephen Rodefer

prose fetishes

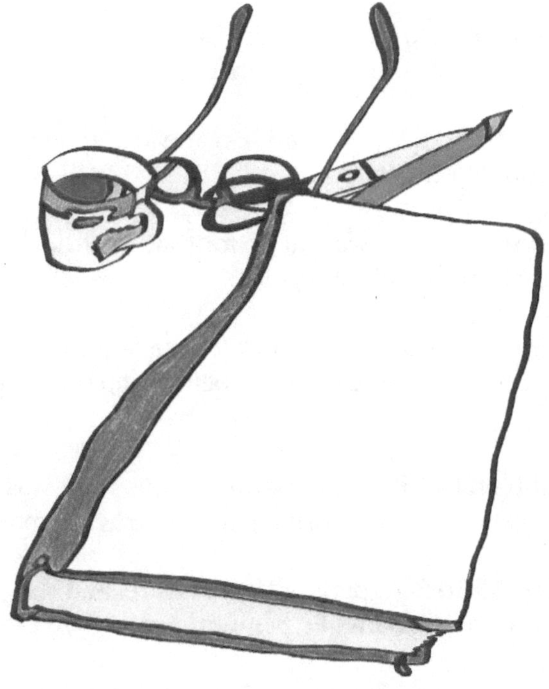

WALL DREAM

for Ann Quin

The white-washed wall in another light. The one vivid dream. The Sadhu priest before me. His shoulder an extension of a tiger's rump. He sits cross-legged. Backs of hands on knees. His body light blue. Sacramental ash. Beard down to his groin. The dream in bed. Lights ascend the white wall. Record player turntable? No reflections from the plastic reel on the tape recorder. Quick bands ascend two walls. Recording. Mozart's C-Major piano concerto for her.

She sat on the hill rock and stared at the photograph of the priest. Lights canceled other lights. To shift your eyes brings back the colors. The orange disk. Of caste? On his forehead. Breasts covered with hairs. Third fingers thick as cocks. Held toward her. She floated. She was high.

Now. The priest simply presides over the door that makes my desk. A large one. I am doing something for someone. Copying these records she likes. Will take the tape over to her. The *123 123 123* movement in the second movement becomes *1* 2 3 4 5 6 7 8 9 10 11 12. One finger can play a melody. Another, a bass.

In my dream I am in bed and can't move. Hear voices. Friends outside. Do they think I'm not here? I move. Very slowly. Exhausting just moving out of the bed. Along the wall. See that I am high. The wall. Is the color of all sound. The warmth of screens in summer. Flies cling to. I see screen upon screen moving. Moire patterns. Chromatic changes. Changes. Must look to see. Think of looking then let 'er rip.

Have I any will over what I see with my eyes closed. Or in the dark. Curtains. I pass. Seeing where I must be. My own living room. People sitting around like they always are. Hanging on beer bottles and waiting. Mine is to enter. Walk to a man with purple bands across his bare skin. I touch his upper arm. HE KILLED HIMSELF BECAUSE YOU TOUCHED HIM. Red-violet comes off on my fingers.

She isn't out on the rock. She saw a man with one arm. Where the other arm should be. Illuminated beetles. She got in the gold Chevy and drove off. Gravel sounds for a long time. She sits and works several hours a day. Waits for me to make this tape of music. Mozart, Beethoven, Erotica, Ahmad Jamal, Archie Shepp, Bach, Bach, Benny Golson, James Brown, Lord Buchly.

Much drinking and dancing that night at the Thunderbird Bar. Room for a lot of laughs. She eyed the bracero with the mustache. Asked him to dance. The man who came over to ask my wife ha! to dance. Lingered on. His hair recently cut off but had some grass back at his house. Said you like this place. You like this place? I hate it. Work awhile and leave. I'm wild. Treat me nice or I'll beat you and your friends up.

Wall. The dream.

Looking through the back window of the car. I am in a boat. Trying to turn my head around. Like trying to get out of bed. But I don't really want to see what is ahead. Only gone by. I am back in the living room walking along the wall. I see all nature. Growing. In the wall. I am back in bed. Looking down at me trying to move. Sun moves. In yellows through the window. The curtain. The morning blows in. I can't move. At once I move my hand and I see it move. I know that I am awake.

That occurs again in knowing my eyes are the screen. Closed to see, open. I can walk. Maneuver. I've been cleaning house. And recording all day. /12Oct66

PRE-CONCEPTION

Joy had the like conception in our eyes
And at that instant like a babe sprung up.
Shakespeare in *Timon Of Athens*

A FRIEND'S LETTER

"The Way encompasses one . . . more part of my life accepting the woman in me. Wrote a letter to Sandy unmailed yet about this on LSD. The next day came into town . My mother very sick. She's fine now after a coma. The woman in me is my mother, made clear by contact with her that day, me on a hill, her in a coma. She's much better now." – Jeff

PISCES WOMEN

Now that she's dead I'm in her memory, what was left in time, my own mother. "The motion of the afterlife," to quote a quote. The greatest female sculptor of all time was Pisces, I think. I give you the given and you grind it to powder, fleabane and sorghum, it doesn't matter what. Take all the instruments and focus on what you're doing, laser beams from all locations in a sphere, your basket in the center where your head is. Your subject is flowers and a photographer. Sculpting with flat visual planes. I lie on the land she photographs, terribly focused parts of it slide by, slide pushed in and out. You make it, fuck, to find my body, sculpt. Head-hunters go quietly to bed. We all feeling the same way and love following the Way perfectly like a road following a road, erasing my own past, putting it down. Set free. Photograph the ghost of her, anti-mother, Pisces, swimming in no death. Mother faced with her hair faded and her body full of water, strain on the heart, alive again in the motion of where we're going. Inertia, 5 senses, inaccurate, organic. Everything shows. Anti-images bleed through the hermetically-sealed coffin, casket (basket). The head-hunters yodel and tear off their buttons, awake for the escape into the night. Fuck where half a mountain is torn off, coming, it is one and the same.

Seeing a fear from all sides, a rock, a rail-trestle, Toltec faces in her photographs. Photograph, the flesh we swim out of. There is my fear sitting on a hill one hill away, up and back, each time easier encompassing being encompassed like stroking into a young woman's vagina. Forever on a hill I lie under, the master half torn away, the rest covered with gas and burned, half a body, a head, mountain, rainbow lying along the ridge and into the canyon. Her coming brought it, rain

after a dry spell, and people running around at night, not dancing, stoned in and out in the head, argument between the dead, image in her.

My body takes off in hers. Is it. I find somewhere along the road in town, reasonably infinite. Near the plot line of the life he thinks he's the master of, the master in a basket that leap-frogged over bridges, as a gift from her, reverses in the mirror, the explosion learning to relax, all these questions on my shoulder. Logs for me to build a house. Digging the foundation, level it and make a dirt floor.

Fear of her photographs of myself. Has never photographed a person, only me. Carrying in the dirt, plants and their shadows, entrance, entrance in the quiet where the meeting rocks us, lying under the motion. On which side of the world? Drop off, dangle out there, seeing it from all sides, destroyed in the image made. Next to her, duplications in the ocean-bush, that swam out of the ocean and became my mother's c . . . Pisces and Pisces looking out of each other's eyes.

Rocking is the motion, ghost of it, two heads arguing in a bush. Flame up the water of the body, dropsied and one-lunged, 30 years of suffering, tuberculosis, *my mother,* died alive, now that I'm of her.

(Dear Ann, whoever heard of flowers arguing – from mother, from friend, from wife)

A light to keep on your head,
keep blowing out of the dead,
mama high over the surf,
calling.

I have given seeds to the world to hold in their hands. Seeds with memories planted in the sea caps, swell, to bounce through the ears. Sing-song from the heart of the kelp, soup I eat, drink, shake the heart. The seeds rattle.

MEXICO

From the shore, riding breakers, the Pacific palms. Mexico comes back through the calendar of fish, their hearts hanging out. Puerto Escondido and the pages are full of sand, thumb prints, arguments left behind, raucous public, address and scratchy mariachis. Long to handle long to firm where we were, Oaxaca. Fish with lime juice, green chile caught at either end by a Pisces woman, Pescado on the rocks, we dashed and roared. Give me lesion to be God all day, and not just where the seeds come out of my body planted in myself herself my love lies, in the capital of memory where *of* is destroyed, and metaphors are drowned. I draw another word.

The hermit comes back from the cave in the ocean to where he left his woman, the love in the room beside the palms and a man in New Mexico, tossed glitter to the 6 directions and sat down on the rock to think, overlooking the last land permitted him to breathe, casting spells in seeds, out of Mexico.

The magic is unconscious, exercised in gestures, the dance in love. When will the ocean come here, lap at his feet, the King of Cups, wandering orgy, his hands in the silence of the mountain, the wind cups hollow laughter and tells him of the girl who caught the largest fish in the ocean, and found the largest rock unphotographed forever, the waves dash against it, classic spray and the sun colors all the clouds back in New Mexico, the piñon jay flies toward a three-quarter moon, her name?

A rabbit flung at the moon, left her imprint.

SON TO BE

There in the bed, have a son, I assumed would be a daughter, the seeds are calling, break all formality of fear where the legs cross, getting into it again the well-tempered clavier, from the photograph. Hermit shows the light for someone to follow, the generation born skips a generation, picking up from the way before, over this mountain bathed in the sacred spring, gold light of sunset. A thousand blues in the dome of sky do not argue among themselves or with it, nor the flowers out there, yellows all over Peyote Rock promontory, jut out over the mesas of the Indians' land, usin's trying this and that too.

Born of alcohol into the blood of the sacred plant, juiced there to have a son the trips tell me, the woman out of the ocean wraps the fish together at my loins, blesses my Gemini heart with her hands and waves at the moon. Her name?

Out of the end of summer, directions given, directions surpassed where communities of l-o-v-e shoot dogs, my dog I've had 4 years, black beautiful half-lab, half-pointer, gone dead for killing chickens. 'Will I ever learn to love,' did the guy with the gun ask, who could have called me to retrieve – Espada.

Keep blowing out of the dead, our brains out on the line drying, new food for generations, to skip a beat, the heart from the sea speaks, her name? The hermit asks. I am myself, intertwined, sing-song, come back from Mexico with her, in love with the woman who caught me, drawing back from full moon, give in, rest on plenty. Water under my chair ends up at the pregnant woman's feet, androgyne or not, and not at the high priestess' till I come back from mating. To the altar on the hill behind my house over looking land we give in to grow out from and back, where ancestors' homes mingle in the rocks, Indians' with mine, and speak through the lights around the head.

I carry in my arms the need, even on high jangling frequencies of man and woman edges, to fall back down where the bed rocks instead of the ocean, without any ruling out, one first altar, grown out of the 2. First. Essence in cloudy myth. Mist breathes over the altar. 2, 2, 2. And then we are 3, in a family. /Jul-Sep 1968

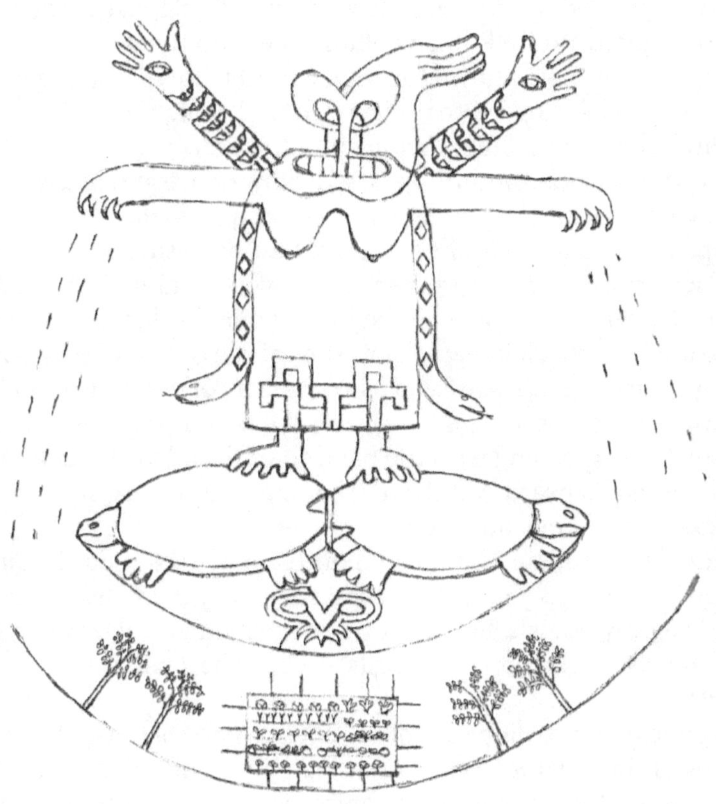

NOTE

The friend is Jeff Sheppard who I met in San Francisco and who visited me in 1968. When I met Lenore she did steel sculpture and photography receiving her Masters at University of New Mexico. After *A New Land* I cashed in a small life insurance policy and we went on a bus trip to Mexico dealing day by day with knowing no Spanish, a pilgrimage to see Coatlicue, Aztec sculpture, pre-Columbian art and sites. We married in December and our son Joel was born the following November.

BIO-RIO

ROSWELL

Wanting a saxophone and denied, it turned out to be drums I played, and back to the piano. So I mowed the lawn on Missouri Avenue while *blasting the Emperor Concerto* out through the screen door - take that! Wanting to practice jazz chords on the piano *until asked to stop.* Small town in Little Texas – as the insult goes.

A hay kiss sock hop barber pole erected. Julia Bapp, the six foot tall Southern Baptist. White Roman columns held up the porch roof of the largest church in town known for cookies and jello salads, and not letting Terry Kyle's fingers, that played Saturday night dances, go near the Church organ on Sunday. Spam church with white columns. No. Terry, you've poisoned your fingers with slow dance and jitterbug music. Don't go near the pipe organ you - play so well.

A Spanish surname Gonzales. Louis, best male singer in Roswell High. I accompanied him and then tap dancers singing *Side by Side.* And *After the Ball* with Betty Boellner bellowing out the dance hall lyrics. And the tall blond jock knew to *blow* the candle out at a Friday school assembly joking,"That's what you learn from a college education." A dance with pompoms and giggling from the first dirty jokes, on the Greyhound Bus speeding with the band to Carlsbad, or Portales, with Harold who had a beard and shaved, kissing Tommy Jeanne under a newspaper – trombone and trumpet players.

"I come to speak for your dead mouths." Pablo Neruda. Talking for Gertrude Stein leaves you in shambles, very witty if you like a young face and slightly bullish. But we never met which isn't why we're still friends. Books cracked open my resistence to the small town strangulation.

It's gone on since high school in America and that huge ball with hundreds of tiny mirrors pasted on it, hanging from the ceiling over the grand piano on the stage in the assembly room used without chairs for dances, and the ball hung up reflects a thousand particles of light, in it seeing the green of the heat moving, always changing in a constant rotation from classes of Spanish and civics and physics to rehearsals and skits and music and put-ons forming the whole school entertainments.

ALBUQUERQUE

Photography since Walker Evans has a downhill news grind which bottoms up in pleasure of the new porno slices of life. That is where it's different from painting, "painting looks like something & photography does not." *Everybody's Autobiography* by Stein. A photographer says, "I've lived in New Mexico 3 years and haven't done a thing, I'm trying to make a film of my goat."

"How hard it is to be oneself and see only what is there!" Fernando Pessoa as Alberto Caeiro. Miss Stein is continually trying to get off the ground and in doing so discovering ground. So the ground is the first place of up. Anything beginning is thronging at the door, the popular, the crispy arrogance of nouveau riche, qualities that suffuse a narrative. "Always the song – waiting to sing." Sherwood Anderson.

Albuquerque in the wind with so many smells today. I was wondering with them to buy bagels, plain, onion and pumpernickel. Then to pay Niki the babysitter for Joel's burned feet and swimming, 10 dollars, and to buy 8 bags of polyester fiber stuffing for Lenore's snake and toys, Solarcaine, super Ektachrome film, beer, milk, bread, a farm jigsaw puzzle for Joel, with farmer and farmer's wife, a peach tree, a kid, a goat, a water pump, a rose bush, a cow, a dog, a farmhouse, a barn. Particles of peculiar mathematics in the pocket on his Osh Kosh overhauls, what do you put in it? Almost 4 years old and studying symbols since everything was one, soaring into the man he might be, ages juxtaposed and drops of sweat rolled down from my right writing arm just fresh from the shower and the humming genius there, feminine, a counter to a male muse. Where was I in this trio of trios, this guna of gunas – Juxta! a friend shouted years ago as he found sacred cows were also scared ones. The little boy, the wife in the shower, the rainbows, the fresh new drawings on her desk with flying impossible birds, my insanity on an even plane as I startled customers rushing in to buy more symbols in even more expensive books.

Dreamed a standard dream last night. Forget mainly what you've been taught. At last a cocktail answer with tail as its cock and Cocteau's tail. How restricted am I in building castles to the moon?

A sentence is a free pleaser. And the emotional plan'll put it together. "Oh yes," the hippy said, "let's get it together," and so we have the finest yogurt now we ever had. How many of my high-school graduating class of '53 now eat yogurt? Only old health freaks which were always somebody's great aunt in California, or them damned Seventh Day Adventists. And Jehovah's Witness right across the street from the Synagogue. Synagogue sounds big, it was a little frame structure.

A SMALL HOUSE LOAN

He was dressed in a recently cleaned and pressed western suit, you know, with the yoke across the back of the coat, and cowboy boots, an appropriate athletic build but with curiously beaked nose, blond and efficient, just back from vacation, desk piled with papers on the third floor of the Albuquerque National Bank. Right next to the Xerox machine, Vice President Oscar Maylon Love, Jr. about my age, loan officer recommended by my father, with bearing from the middle class world, and his father was OM Love, President of the bank. Help, to build our house. Yes.

Last night I dreamed there was water that swelled through the house till it flowed through walls and swallowed our possessions and moved them out dissolving the adobe. I found that my poems, things I made and all her things too, were safe and some how dry again in plastic bags. The night before I was dropping straight down in a car, a vertical road which all turned to water falling and then flattening out into a river. I was in the middle flowing. /Jun-Sep73

INTRO FOR A DUO READING

Bill Pearlman and Steve Rodefer

Bill and Steve - Lenny Silverberg in back

Fervent Valley is old New Mexico Fruit, *Oriental Blue Streak*, Dr. Amer-Indian Negro Woman Chicana Duende White Brother spelled backwards, and Bill Pearlman whose Age is Apparent, and Steve Rodefer whose manner Takes the Cake – something to do with D. H. Lawrence and Robert Creeley, Georgia O'Keefe, William Eastlake and the Indian on the Hill – John Rechy, Keith Wilson and Others and Others and *Space* – WHICH IS UNDER THE SUBTERRANEAN REACHES OF OKIES BAR and this building – Placitas, Corrales and Beyond the Visionary Artaud Hirschman Kinetic in Pealrman – he drops down acid rhetoric in contrary planes and Rodefer as Voices carries lovemaking, the *Sight* which is inner Province of Troubadour in spillage careful outward – these Two Gents of Lore around this town – all part of a renewed face of the Southwest. In 1967 Zingdap! & I fell down the stairs by the orchestra pit into the arms of six beautiful women – & I have nothing better to urge on this evening but the entire possibility of Speech in Dance of Reform of itself – friends & all – *Steve Rodefer & Bill Pearlman!* /73

FAMILY PORTRAIT

for Joel and Lenore, Brewster and Clem

In that Valley, a different colored string from each finger, so that one of another, each knew the other, in Love's Dream *eh*-stablished, higher lower fiery icy headed, empty headed in, come, come the Serpent round the Sun, the *S's* from seen Heaven – Spillway, Rainbow. Joel Ai Rainbow, Son Bird, holding Brewster, Feline, watching Clem Moonrider, the Pointer, pup. Full Hill landless Lord over Laughter, he saw him tricking the Sun, the Father Bird, Yoked Poet, holding hidden Bowl of Ometéotl, and other times the Staff, or Book. Under Whirl around the

Sun in vacuum-headed, icy quest, search out, find in leg of the Valley the dip in Care for Fam-I-ly, Family – portion spread out from Her touch, strung hair, Fishless Hair, Pisces, morning sewing, drawing, whirl in birth of swimming headdress, wood on wood, birds flying to the star under many circles, serpents all tied to the ends of rainbow strings from his fingers, passing, as I say, to her voice, passing through his, wood on wood knocking.

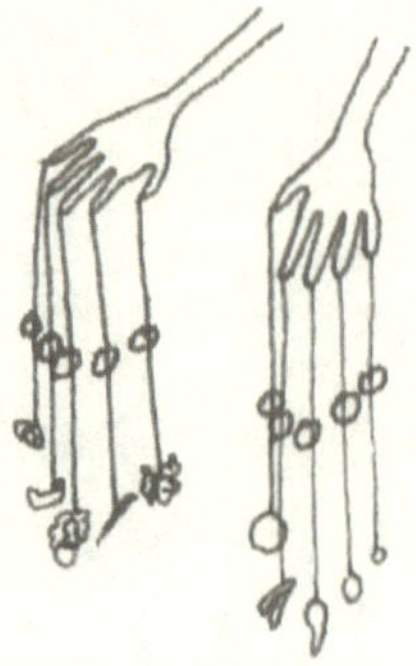

The country is blind and the land he needs for a house to grow up on for the son, and all, her hand, constant voices interrupted, tied together going out in seen through eras – March, June, November, and Soon. Seeing it, it is all too sugary – let us have Sight.

A little bag of sugar, a larger one of salt, one of chile and all Earth's pleasures, one of bones to bang against each other in prayer, one of winds, the thumb almighty, one of little Mudheads trying to emerge, one of a stick pointing direction, one of fertility – red leaf lettuce – one of awkward hesitation, an empty cradle. And the last, the little finger from the Rainbow string, the center of the Ear, and hearing what you see.

I see my hands and the garbage on the wall, opening the spaces where the eyes can behold her wonder and his there where it is directed, and coming back in dreams we oughtn't to cling to – who knows? "Prefer the Unknown" where the colors come down in the Spring. December burning and burning on the head, over the head, into full light. /9Dec73

TRAVELING TO SCARBOROUGH

(from my donut seat)

Having never seen them my mind explodes its immature rest. Traveling pictures, the Crypt of Lastingham Church, from Scarborough. How do you get to Europe, how do you get up and move when the Furies pull you down, New Mexico Furies with their cottonwood tops and snake bottoms. How do they land. How do you frame the economic picture, have someone over for dinner when the dinner party doesn't get off the ground. How do you get off the ground. The mind moves, enlivens each dead fingernail. How do you trim them, how can you tell when you're peeing when you're peeing and not asleep dreaming you're peeing on the local boundary stones, Prick in the Thorn, Prick in the Stone Stoop, and Saddle Rock. Beginning again the "H" in history, "I" is a story and the bedrock faints under the lack of language. Living outside the boundary stones, *never* attending Scarborough Fair, the bathing vans and hokey-pokey, sailing trips from bay to bay, Fol-de-Rol in the Floral Hall.

The mind stops and sinks into the ground where it belongs, they tell you, whistling at your back, bunching up in rainbows to egg you on. Why go to Greece, why go to Wood End, overlooking the Valley Gardens, the former home of the Sitwell family largely devoted to wild life, Scarborough's natural history museum. Especially interesting are the living creatures in the vivarium. The Sitwell Wing is kept much as the family knew it when they spent holidays there, Sir Osbert, Dr. Edith, and Sacheverel Sitwell. To grow old is to grow more odd is a young person's view. Dr. Edith did it. At USC when she visited and lectured. When the young man in fearful respectful distance broke the silence and moved up close around her, she proved warm without mistaking, and the rustling of her gowns let out moths over his head.

Stuffy statues aren't my bag in those forbidding entrance halls, but Richard III's house? Café and Bar? Stained glass windows and full body armor? I visit the traveler's guide.

Caedmon's Cross carved with an unlettered herdsman's "Song of Creation" composed one night in his dream, earned him the title Father of English Poetry. In Hilda's time 1300 years from now the stones Hilda turned from snakes to stones, Whitby ammonites, will turn back into snakes and closer to home, my reality, the trinitite from Trinity Site outside Alamogordo will turn back into sand and the 1945 Mushroom Cloud overhead will disappear in blind people's heads as they go to sleep, and Coxwold Village, where Tristram Shandy was completed, will draw up Laurence Sterne's water for his morning bath, as I wave goodby to the memory of myself on the door plate visiting the visitors somewhere outside Scarborough, somewhere deep interior castle walls where someone passed by before America became named absurdly, the fathers of my brain and mothers of my body, traveling again, to ease this daily hurting, contained where I am, the bird that calls the wind around me when I talk to the grass plants through the scarlet runner beans, the bird inside my body wants to try out its wings. /4Oct75

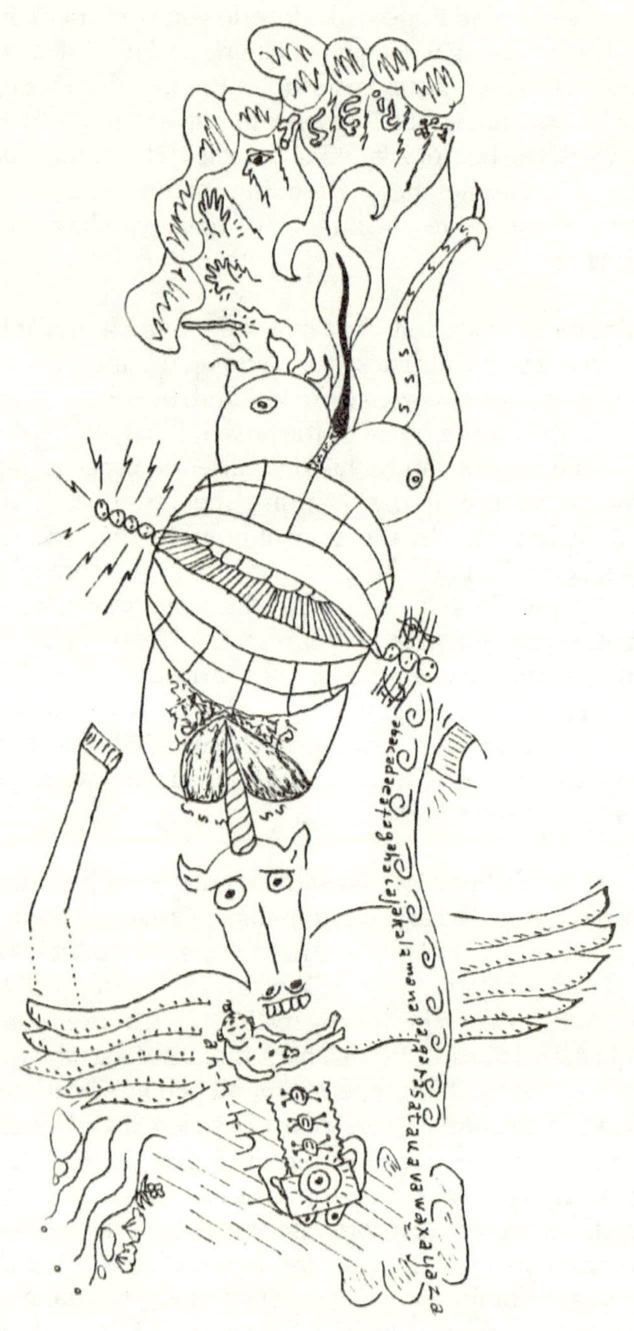

(from “The Birth of Poetry broadside 1981 lg)

POETO'S HOUR

Poeto took pen to paper. There was a shuffling in the other room but all fell silent. The scratching of the pen echoed down the canyons of immortality. This was what he said or sang as he wrote:

"Ladies and Gentlemen, My pen is big." The scratching echoed out there to the chickens. "The revulsion I've lived through has not passed. So long I've hated you and thought you were sheer nylons with me trying to fill your bag. I've blown you and blown you and still not blown you down. You're bigger than me by a long shot. You have toes – and ears – and fights. You fight me. You jam your nylon stocking over my head. I love it. I wish I had one on my head now. I wouldn't look at you. I'd eat you. You eat me up. You gag on my face, but you're little. Little than big. Bigger than a toenail. You're gas stations and the whole rigamarole up to the top. I am the top of the pyramid. Blinking the eye on your goddamn dollar bill. You're mammon and a preacher. You have free time on Sundays and tend your garden club. Your radio audience isn't fixed, your radio audience is all you've got and it's free. Free to move over and let me take a stand.

"Eat whole foods. This is your radio audience listening. Listening to the Poeto give his fireside chat. There is rain in Cambodia. The Communists have fallen and picked themselves up. They are crazy with laughter. They have bifocals too. They've heard of Benjamin Franklin. They want him to come over and buddy buddy with them. They've restored the locks in the canals. The voices are pulling your head apart. Don't jam them any more. Don't screw them in any further. You are totally nuts and I hate your guts. You are the Nazis. You are not this radio audience.

"I have not said anything trivial, that's why you hate me. You might listen to me but you're married. You have kids that glue their heads together out of nothing to do. You would let Gertrude Stein die of a miscarriage. Baudelaire is your Uncle. And Edgar Allen Poe. You make sense to me because you're instant art. You're constantly echoing in the hills of Congress all over the land. Until you fall silent. You are hung over and don't know it. I can't destroy you and I love you. I bid you walk for me. *Get up and talk for me.*

"I am potentially your victory. Your victim and your victory. But reaching out I grab you. There's peace in the Yucatan. Fighting is calm over Alaska. There are marching girls in Paris. No one wears stockings any more. What a thing to deplore. This is your midnight speech on

Sunday. We need more wire fence. To fence ourselves out, away from you. You dogs. *You dogs.*

"You bottom dogs. Sooner or later you will meet your failure. Failure to do this or that. I will play your game until *you* play it. Play it all the way up where I'm the floating pyramid. I am all the gurus in the top shelf. I am Carlos Castaneda's hand on backwards. Clapping ass and calling me pardner. You are dissolving in Alka-Seltzer, Hadacol and Sal Hepatica. Pow! When hate disappears isn't it great? What a beautiful day this is. Everything is balmy and there isn't any noise. Sometimes somebody forgets to do something but they're paying me to talk tonight. I'm selling you a bill of goods. Vote for Crazy Horse the Doctor of Medicine. Be kind to your families and try to include a Poet in your social acquaintances. Ask him a question about God, or grass. Promote the use of useless electricity? Use the electricity that is to be used. And no more. Make garbage bags your grab bags and give them away in public. Sit down at somebody else's plate and eat his food every disgusting drop of it. Smell your own manure wastes and don't heap scorn on somebody else's plate. But you will do this anyway. Dear God let us pray.

"We pray and we pray and pray. And still the plants come up. We can't wish them away so we pray and we pray and we pray. Dear God how we pray. We play and we pray. Don't you, fig, come up. I want only weeds in my garden. Social weeds. Weeds that fuck each other while I can stand by and catch fire. This is your poet talking to you, your small town farmer poet. The poet tilling the soil and turning the soil under your feet. While you march along together. Trampling it down. You stepped on my bind weed. I am your *living* weed. I am the history of natural flowers. I stop where your nylon stocking starts. I am the You of the nation. A living legend in trees. I am your walking Campus. I am your inspired parts. I wait for the wave of inspiration. It comes and comes and comes, and makes me the prize winner. The winner of your Emmy Poet Award. Nineteen Seventy Sixty Two. I am the you of the me of the sea. The sea is talking tea tonight. Salty teardrop tea. I am the puff in you're a Bomb smoke. I am making your money, I am giving you all the angles, I am half again a man. A man on top of man is stronger too. The woman of my dreams passes through. Through *here!* Right here this minute, you filthy scads. Try out my dreams. I'll hand you the box that contains them. Sniff well.

"Your mind reaches out to shake my hand. Here is the ten bucks. Call me again when you want to write a poem. I'll pay you a decent wage for services rendered. I am your public. This is a musical interlude. I am your employer. John Q Public.

"You write me a poem for my wedding and we'll give you a crisp new 10 dollar bill. I love you, Peggy Sue. I take the woman on my left to be my hip and sway. To be the one I live today, to love and wish away and dine and dine and dine. Dine. And day. A dime a day keeps the apple away. Avoid doctors unless they read a poem every day. Sometime. Read this poem Doctor and read this poem Doctor AMA, your heart is not in the right position. We will move it over here and beat against the rib cage our message here tonight. Avoid white sugar. Fill up your stomachs with praise. *Read* more. Do more outside work but not of too regular a fashion. Or you'll get in the rut of your stereotype and become sane. You want to remain a weed. A weed in my very special garden. Yes you are you, and you are you. Listen to the cloud forming above you. Try out your sixth sense but not in any organized way. Rotate the voices inside you. Listen to me I am you, in me the way I am. This is the way I am you're paying for inspiration. *Constantly* risk and you'll be extending with me. More more more is not necessarily fattening. By demanding more you are extending yourself into a thin presence.

"Don't ever say what has been said before. Let me repeat. Don't ever allow yourself not to listen when you ask me a question. Listen to your answer, but in my head. And we truly will become partners. I will report the news as I see fit. I will announce the presence of the iceberg, or pyramid, as you wish. The solid object of my voice falls like a lump at your feet. A furry body. You pick it up. It sings. It says, there is value in my voice while I'm still alive. Don't kill me in order to pick my guts. Show me how we can think a thought together. I can be your synapse, because you are listening. You are listening to me tonight. Thank you for listening to *me*, listen."

Shut up. /28May76

In commemoration of KUNM-FM's stronger voice, which can now be heard in Placitas, I read this, in part, over the air during the L.G. Show May 1976.

BATHTUB INTERVIEW WITH POETO

(transcribed from a tape running while in the tub)

"The avant-garde has been made up, I think, completely, and all through history, with people who are bored by other people's ideas."

Frank O'Hara

Are human beings restricted?

"Human beings live conscious of immediate barrier-like surroundings which only enclose so much space. That's why art galleries or museums are still viable, because the concept of a museum or gallery is that you can walk into a restricted space, I mean you know what's going on on the other sides of the gallery walls, and be transformed. Which relates directly to a Japanese tea garden where you can blot out the traffic noise and sights and city goings-on by just stepping in this area which is surrounded by trees, and step into a room which is surrounded by wood, and really understand what it's like to read about or see something you have never experienced.

(Bathtub Water Noise)

"The secret of any kind of enter-able event is its restriction in space. If it didn't have that restriction in space it wouldn't be as powerful, therefore you can be content with the friends you have. But the problem with contentment is that it's an ideal, and everybody wants to make new contacts all the time. So some make new "friends" faster than others, others take a long time to make good contacts. And then there is the difference between two people concerning the definition of friendship and whether or not your contact is really an acquaintance or just a friend. But I have never been able to find out who a friend is, because friend is an ideal and it remains as an ideal, and is occasionally touched on by reality.

"I think the true friends are the ones that are with you the most whoever they may be, how many there may be, that when you're by yourself, that's the true test of friendship. That could only be for a few minutes in a particular day say, that you're completely by yourself, surrounded by the room that you're in at the time, or the sky outside. Then is when yon can best define friendship and know who your contacts truly are, because generally they will come to you, one after the other, as friends in your mind, and if you are reasonably content at that time, it's like watching a zodiac of people you know well, and trust and love, knowing that within each category of trust there are deleterious wanderings along the way, zigzags from the ideal, as those big words always are ideals. And love, whether you consider friendship to be companionship or love, sex-love, friendship will continue to be friendship. Friendship will generally be when you're talking about something very important to both of you, very important, and it's also simultaneously very important that both of you are talking about it, and it seems almost a secret as you're talking about it. That's the test of friendship when you are with your friend, not when you are away from her, or him, or it.

"10 years later you may not be seeing that friend anymore, and you've heard such and such has happened to your friend and it seems like you are very far away from this friend, but you don't particularly miss this friend because so many things have happened and you've made new friends."

(Bathtub Water Noise)

Mr, Poeto, would you mind telling us what you think about performance.

"Everybody performs all the time. Oscar Wilde said "Appearance is all." It is up to you to change it if you want to. If you don't like your appearance change it, it's as simple as that. A couple red checks on each cheek, a little hydrogen peroxide on a lock over your forehead. Just think (it's like) a little swish and sway with Danny Kaye. Or Aikido Now, Forever, or Judo, or writing books about subduing mastodons, or just an increased interest in Egypt. I think that America's history has led to the final awareness, though all awarenesses are final. America's history has led to one shining development – the hobby. That's where America can be seen at its best. In the hobby sections of all the fairs, and there's one coming up here. Now my hobby is carrying on an interview while taking a bath. I find it quite modern to do that, actually it's decadent that's why I call it modern. The things which I really value in my life I classify as contemporary. Modern to me is a really old-fashioned term. It's probably showing up in antique stores now, and there certainly is a boom in antiques.

"Most of my interests have now become antiques. There's a hell of a lot of me that is definitely saleable, however there needs to be a name for my saleable product and I haven't quite figured out whether I should call it Larry Goodell Specimens, or simply an attribute of someone we all love. For instance, if you're really bored, why don't you start collecting knotholes. Knot-holes are fascinating because they go in a different direction in their grain, than the wood that they are within, so they leak moisture like mad, and you have to seal them a lot if you're sealing them, *and* the knotholes that are windows. I've always felt a special affinity with knotholes, especially when the knots are in them. It bothers me a little more if the knots have fallen out, because to identify with a knothole when the knot has fallen out, is much more difficult and vacuous a thing to do, at least for me . . ." *(recording ends)* /25Aug76

✣

POETRY AND ETIQUETTE - POETO

"The first thing you do in a book of etiquette is ask yourself 'Is it permissible?' and when you answer yourself that it is, you go ahead and do it anyway. Of course it is. It is okay to send money to a person in lieu of a gift if you are unable to buy a gift and send it. It's cheaper to send money than packages anyway. Go ahead and do it. If someone serves you a knife a fork a spoon pointed toward you go ahead and turn them back the way they're supposed to be. Your host may be some Sufi-Sikh witch doctor who was raised in Lower Slobovia, New York, and is trying to influence you. Laugh and eat, and get out of the situation.

"If you get there too late and all the food is gone think that you might have been poisoned anyway, and when they're out of beer don't drink the tap water, it will make you sick. Think of your planning not to drink and how awful it is once you're all geared up to drinking. Everything ends and the day comes anyway.

"'On the Wings of Song,' dropped, by them onto the earth.
Will absurdities ever
end yes they
will yes they
will when you
come back down to
Earrrrrrrrrrrrrrrrrrrrth.

"Dare to think it is possible to do what you are going to do, and do it. A bulwark was never spent by a theft. Three cheers for the function and one for the category. Think your head through, and back to the other side.

"Poetry is an exercise in thinking thoughts, music in the ears. You walk down the passage of your ear canal and back out again. You bless your wife your son your daughter your house your ideal construction looking out on a volcanic stem like an upside down mushroom, and when you see the rainbow is no longer there hard rock reality gets to you.

"Etiquette is the carrying on of the mind. It gets to where it's going and passes through space. Do what is right no matter what. Etiquette is harder than poetry. Carrying yourself without demanding that you dominate everything, unless of course you deserve to, dominating it anyway. That's the opposite of poetry. Poetry is when you don't care, etiquette is when you care but don't give a damn. Poetry is a wall that's breaking through. Etiquette is a dam held back. Amy and Emily handed you a bejeweled hand with long polished fingernails. Now you put on your kid glove and handle things carefully. Don't let not knowing something stop you, but admit your ignorance without going too far. There's a stepping stone anywhere as long as it's on your property, and if you don't have any property you can still walk.

"Go ahead and do what you thought you couldn't do, by doing it. Bit by piece, a lot. Bite off a huge chunk every day and don't give anything away, until you have reached where you're going and are there.

"That's the difference between etiquette and poetry – one's coming and one's going. Do you really live on such a pint-sized shelf that you can't listen to something odd. Have you ever been startled by anything? Of course you have, you just can't remember.

"What's wrong with the public schools? The only poetry in them is under the desk. That is, if poetry bit her between the legs she'd probably scratch her ear. Most teachers are just so much wet soap as far as poetry goes. There are younger ones, just as they are younger doctors and lawyers, but they won't speak of poetry and etiquette in one breath. Perhaps they never will. I will go on and do what is present to do. Today we have a list.

Write San Diego.
Write Ecuador.
Write the insurance company.
Run off postcards announcing your radio show.
Send them.

"Be friendlier all the way around. Perhaps that will help. Think of others as your mind boggles, work solidly without interruption. Work and play, etiquette and poetry. Poetry is so easy, it's the aftermath that's questionable. Poetry should be called afterbirth. By constantly beginning you are constantly ending your former task. That way, truthfully, you can reach your way out and still be a family unit. Stepping apart, and then everybody wins.

"Doing something gracefully, falling, gracefully into bed, or say, standing up, walking. Dancing. Poets should dance, all the time, set them to dancing. Be kind and truthful. Why not. Because you're a perfect devil?

“Language will teach you things you never knew, and why not? Sex guides the words, home. Or accepts them, at an emotional pitch, or tosses them back. But ride with the day.

“I am Emily Post's vacuum system. Actually I'm making fun. I hope I entertain, but if I don’t call me Arbuthnot, or some old thing. Still dinner was wonderful and took so much preparing. Our garden passes through our mouths and down into the empty canals there. Generously we help each other with our selves through our lives. The evening learned something from it.” /14Aug77

A FABLE OF THE POOR

Once there was a man who had a diamond. The diamond was so big that it would glow in the dark. The man took the diamond everywhere, he wore it on his left hand and he never stumbled. A poor neighbor with better eyes saw him walking down the road at night with the diamond on his hand lighting the way. The poor neighbor was envious and he robbed the man in the night knocking him down dead in the road. The poorer neighbor then put on the diamond and wore it down the road. He could see everything and it was wonderful. He never stumbled though he'd never stumbled before. His eyes were very good and he didn’t need the diamond that glowed in the dark.

His neighbor, poorer than him saw him walking down the road illuminated by the diamond. He was envious like the other man was and he rose up before him in the glow and struck him down dead for the diamond. I will sell this diamond and become rich and rich he felt walking down the road all aglow at night. This continued over and over until the poorest man alive saw his dreadfully poor neighbor walking down the road at night wearing the diamond and his path all aglow. I must have that for myself said the world's poorest man, and I will be poor no longer, I am so tired so tired of being poor. He was on the point of striking his neighbor down to get the glowing diamond when his neighbor said Wait I If you strike me down dead then there will be no poor man left on earth for I am rich with this diamond all aglow and you are the last poorest man on earth. And when you have the diamond and are walking down the road in the night with your path all aglow, a rich man not as rich as you-with-this-big-diamond will strike you down dead and there will be no one on earth left who's ever been poor, only a rich person striking down a less rich person to gain the wealth of this glowing diamond. True, said the poorest man on earth, when you and I are dead, there will be no one left who knows how awful it is to be poor, how awful living the poor life is when you're the poorest of the poor, but until I strike you down dead and take the diamond all aglow I shall be the poorest of the poor and living a dreadful life. The other man said, then let us share this diamond walking down the road with our way lit up in the darkest night and rich as we can be with this diamond between us, keeping alive the memory of what it is like to be poor, and when a rich person comes and wants to do us in it will be twice as hard for that person because we are two against one.

So the two men walked down the road at night, one would wear the diamond and hold it out to light their path and then the other would wear it holding it out between them to light the way, and they swapped stories all night long and though they were hungry, the memories of the poor of the planet earth were so many and so fresh alive within them that the stories would never end.

When dawn came, the friends were so hungry that they sold the diamond for a pretty price and divided up the thousands and felt themselves very rich. They sat long over breakfast having the best of coffee and telling stories that no one else had ever heard.

But then one night when they returned to their homes they sat drinking long telling stories of the poor people that no one else had ever heard till one of them that had been the poorest rose up against the other saying you my friend are the murderer for you killed to get that diamond we had, but I never did. And the other said but you intended to kill and would have had I not dissuaded you, and so they calmed themselves down, but it took a long time. And when they died their families wrote down the stories they remembered the two men had told who had been the last of the poor on earth. And this book was entitled the Poorest of the Poor on Earth. And it was bound in emeralds and silver for everyone on earth now had moderate wealth at least and no one went hungry or ill without a doctor and being poor was just a memory someone had from reading in this book, and the name of the book was the Poorest of the Poor on Earth, and it was passed around to all who hadn't read it, and people shook their heads and said, so that was what it was like to be poor on this earth and everyone, everyone alive was glad that being so poor was a thing of the past.

/14Sep77

DEAR EDITORS OF *SEER'S CATALOGUE*

Misconceptions are the rule and the rule of conceptions. Giant letters you jump from when you want to commit suicide. Gowns waving or necklace hitting your nose. No noise, you jump into somebody else's swimming pool which is used for solar heating, unlock the valve and stand there naked as the water drains.

In the dream I conceived of letters to myself half finished because I was only half alive. Now the doctor stuck his finger up my ass and provoked me hard and is convinced I'm mostly okay so I'll finish my first letter.

Dear Editors of the local underground. You scratch the surface. And go on to your next deadline. Scratch the surface and go on, scratching surfaces. One guy's quick comments half quoted representing hundreds in the area? Representing what. Go into the very bottom of the iceberg and float it up before our eyes. Put your flippers on. Your frog masks. Your underwater weathervane. And don't come up for air until you can breathe.

What is written can't be chopped if the writer is a writer. To hell with convention, there is no news except North East West and South. Where are you standing, standing for what. In depth? Certainly not quick as TV. But how deep? How much time do you have before jumping off? The giant letters you're jumping off are ALBUQUERQUE, not HOLLYWOOD, though there is a Hollywood, New Mexico, there's also a Paris, Texas.

Publishing dead news obligates you to give equal time to the live. *I* am the news. As far as I can see you are very conservative, an unused conservancy ditch in disguise. Let's open up the locks and strike dead center. I want you to live, babies. Tap a little closer to the source of creation. But what, where is it if you can't see beyond the nearest ballot box. The more enemies you have, the closer you are to the Source. The Source is Male and Female and has not been revealed, yet, though Sears and Roebuck comes closer than Seer's.

Ever, LG
/resigning as Editor of the "Writer's Page"
in Seer's Catalogue October 9, 1975

MR. PIBB

Everything was electric with the suicide sensuousness of the day. Mr. Pibb bore down the avenue of Central New Mexico leaving all his cares behind. Floating, out of the womb of his home in Dimmsdale outside the city, he was *in* the city and felt higher than a kite. He thought at any moment someone would hand him a slice of apple pie, right down from the sky. There was a rocking to his gait as he walked down from the Coin Laundry across the parking lot of Taco Villa and into the Victory Gasamat. He pulled a nickel from one pocket, a quarter from his laundromat stash in the other, and looked over the vending machine labels – Coca-Cola, Coca-Cola, Sprite, Fanta, and Mr. Pibb. He was startled out of his wits at his name on the vending machine. Mr. Pibb! He dropped the money in, pushed the label and fished out his can of pop. He flipped the top, dropped it in the slot provided for it, and took a careful sip.

Mr. Pibb reminded him of his youth. There was a hint of Royal Crown, or was it Pepsi, in the pseudo caramel taste. He read the label as he walked back to the laundromat. Carbonated water, sugar, may contain dextrose-fructose syrup, caramel color, phosphoric acid, preserved (*what* is preserved) with 1/40th of 1% sodium benzoate, caffeine, artificial and natural flavorings (*that* includes the whole universe), mono-sodium phosphate, and lactic acid. My God! what am I drinking, he thought, and sipped, and this reminds me of my youth? Before I read labels what was in those things I drank? He drank the last sip and dropped the can into the laundromat trash hamper.

/in memory of my father, Lawrence Goodell /4Aug77

GREG TUCKER: "IT'S A RIOT"

/at Meridian Gallery, Albuquerque

Greg Tucker's show at the Meridian dares to show what it's like to be a man, the myth that we all are afraid to face. All of us men. That opening out of hate and love, that is peculiarly masculine, because it is fierce, brutal, and escapes all risks.

It is a show of tattooed men, what you do with your body in prison when there's nothing else to do. Transferred, in simple, bold thrust of minimum color, on small squares of paper. You move from paper to paper, with these images on them. A Christ "Born to Lose," "Fix," "Arbol de Juzgar," etc. And then the images of the penitentiary riot, the messages of directed violence on the walls, kill this guy or that guy, cut off that guy's prick – a show of such manageable drawings, manageable because the drawings aren't that big and the terror diminishes as you walk away, and yet it's not terror. Some drawings are of masks, or bodies without heads, or just a scrawl like a cross-out, on the square of paper, or numbers through 9, backwards.

It is the rage of being independently male, in a body trapped in prison where the puberty rite of the tough edge you only show, comes bursting out. That puberty rite of the tough edge only showing, as you walk along or do anything, the boy-man learns in Junior High. Greg Tucker shows these images of that pushed-out toughness, the lump-in-the-throat terror that we guys have to go through, either do or duck, shit or get off the pot, kill or die – or escape. The escape of the trapped, no matter what they were or who they were, they are, there, climbing the walls to get out.

For art to show this is remarkable – and remain art. It isn't art overridden by statement. I think it is Greg Tucker's sensibility of the pen riot, tattoos, graffiti caught in the process of his own drawing. And the energy continues from them as you look at them. It isn't the stupid knife-edge painless hurt of so many contemporary popular movies, that just make you hurt if you can do that anymore, but the small squares of drawings you enter like entering a cell, to see what goes on in that prisoner's mind or body. And more than that, it is an expression of what all men have to face, suffering all the while through it, a trap door on the way to manhood that can trap you and never let you out. If you get trapped, it's the rigamarole of proving your toughness round and round, egged on by "buddies" that it's okay, until you believe the game and play it till you kill or maim or get back at, as if that would end it, and it never does.

It's a rotten game that few women know, that is at the core of the independent male, who travels through it until some kinder register of what life can be, begins to settle in. These drawings are extremes of what is as common as the human male, a stage of his development, or trapped in itself, the horror of everything gone wrong and every act can only be the further extension of wrong, wrong into wrong, a mass wipe-out.

Drawing by Greg Tucker

But it's only drawing, it's only writing. Drawing, writing on the wall.

/September '80

NOTES ON PERFORMANCE AND NARRATIVE ART

ART NOTES 1

Art is a return to normal, a sliding back of the scale to economy and wise decisions, decisions made in the heat of passion never remembered in tranquility.

It is vinegar and soda mixed and when the froth is over the limp dry aftermath that results.

That's why performance is so interesting. There they pay the performer, you pay at the gate and you go in to be detained for an hour or so. What a relief from the tedium of life to go somewhere and have the intensification of tedium to deal with. The pretense that life is alright and that the froth at the top of the fishbowl means that the fish are having a good time.

While underneath it is murky and reptilian presidents glue jaws on each other and suck each other's last remaining death instincts out.

It is the small presidents that matter that are young these days. Those that get away with creating romance and giving us in the club something to laugh about. We can only start locally unless we're rich and here we are rubbing shoulders with art that makes no noise, pictures that rot in the gardens of the brain vacuums of the artists, noisome pretenses of "what's going on" when most of it is bad painting, sexless cowboy sculpture or decorative purses turned inside out and parading as breasts.

The only return is the strength of the instincts where the quality of remorse is pure and life gets caught in the action. Careful pure draftsmanship with the heart-head in every particle of ink. The flow of pure art is a rare line with wash of meaning connecting or filling. Over a period of time the story builds up until it takes time to "listen," which hardly any of us have. Thus the intense loneliness of the real artists and the terrifying wall-breaking going on, whether you hear it or not.

Narration is all that remains of our personal stories whether anyone listens or not. No drinking bars anymore to string yourself out on somebody else's line. Only the closed bars of a penitentiary culture with the individual raging going on.

✣

ART NOTES 2

Art is living spaces void of contact. Holistic Europa. You rape a rope a Naropa pope. To elucidate is pure luxury. There can never be going back over and defining except in lawyers' offices and therapy. Art therapy is going back over what you've seen. It's healthy, hilarious and holistic. All the holes are present. You are constantly beginning anew whether you like it or not. Art notes. Art notes 2. Too much raging gets boring. Ranting and raving is a cliche and raging turns into song. Curiously delirious song comes up over the walls where you turn and look out the window. Suddenly all is pure. You may define.

Number 1. Performance brings contact back into art. There is the poet's living breath. There is the sense of where the body has been in dance. Your eyes follow the dancer or the movement in the gallery space. But this only happens a little, not a lot. There's always a place for curious static art to borrow the walls and take up space. The register of what is pure for centuries, but it is pure and golden that some few people have better knowing eyes than others. In a city of a quarter-million you may rub shoulders with other artists all the time but the league of the spirit that maximizes strength dissipates when there are so few sure eyes – and exact hands. Hands that are eyes, for instance. When hands are eyes.

The walls take up the space and throw it out the windows. A curiously pure day. Pure New Mexico fall space. We live so few to know. The sun bright and warm through the large windows. The cherry trees red leaves. Yellow brown cottonwoods down in the arroyos. Living here above the town and in the village. The village contours shape the mind. The mind throws out the town and becomes rural. We must be democratic if we are to have any friends. There are too few spaces that are capitalized by greatness. We feed it back into the furrow – bone meal, blood meal, manure. As if I was a plant. My mind is mated to plants. We are crossbreeds. And out of that comes a shape that gives art season. Arts grouped by season. Calendars of art. Poetry, the pushing up of song, the small painting more than the large one, the minuscule defining growing, growing, getting so big it's almost a yard long and a foot wide, her painting. His sculpture a long board with a shoe on it saying Fuck off! Wood grows. Paper grew. Paints came out of the earth on paper. Canvas a weaving you could wear if you were stiff.

✣

A STORY

Europa was made whole by Zeus who made love to her under the plane tree. He carried her off in the form of a beautiful bull over the waters to Crete. Zeus was made whole by all the holes he plugged. Beautiful holy Zeus. Beautiful Europa, holistic Europa, and all the holes are singing they are plugged. The plugged holes sing and the gods are born. Out of them they come, one by one, and sometimes two by two. Heaven and earth give birth. The straining and the lurch. Europe is named. A beautiful bull is blamed. Over the waters to Crete. The white bull's feet tripping over the crests of the waves, Europa on his back flowers falling from his horns and there under the plane tree in Crete made love, leaves bright red overhead. You can see them right now framed against the sky, the bolt blue sky that brings the crisp edge to things.

The imagination pictures pictures before and after the pictures hanging on the wall. And that is narration, seeing pictures that aren't on the wall. The happening between the frames that isn't movies. Movie frames happen faster. Picture frames don't exist in narration, verbal narration. I told or retold a story. You can see it. The crisp leaves of autumn. But in a painting frame after frame telling substance of a person's life, the visualized essence, parade of essences, that is narrative visual art at its best. It is an imagined performance in a life scope caught in the drawing or painting, and you must have a group of them to get the different views of the visual life, superior eyes. Her world given in ecstatic pieces laid out in a pretense of calm color.

Best art is ecstatic, but nobody uses that term, it's stated calm. But behind the calm is the canvas or paper hanging there, perpetually. That is, the counterpoints release the color in rhythms of tension. Tense taut, tense taut. That is its subtlety, the subtlety of Lenore Goodell's painting/drawings. Tense, taut, the color rhythms out through tension, the tension within, hanging caught there, trapped to sing, which is not a raging but a singing, and the life story goes on between and through each picture hanging on the wall. This is not performance but implied performance.

Narrative art is implied performance of the artist going through life, each segment lopping over between each segment. Each "frame" lopping over between each "frame" – until a life is built, that is a vision of it. As complete as any key can be that fits and leads to something. Essence charged whole in parts that sing through tension out. That anyone can look, who likes to look and look – almost with 13 eyes, if you had them, or better yet, one good one, to see it out.

/30Oct-1Nov80

Narrative Art Show, Albuquerque United Artists, downtown and Lenore paintings and others telling stories on the wall.

THE CLUB

With apologies to all **l=a=n=g=u=a=g=e** poets and a blat warp to others.

Language is a flat banana cake that got me up in the morning for the wrong reason. I, being no other than Robert Creeley or Albert Brown or Bert Fielding. Bearing no resemblance to exact pancakes you crossed with mud and gave to Marilyn Pitman as a pat on the back. This plot mystified London when Xerxes had a hardon. It's fun when you're not supposed to be having anything but green paste. Europe crossed its eyes on America's backside humor. Carrion humor. The cat on the table was allergic to the table but sat there, ate there, turned to cold fish. Anyway Herbert said John Lee Hooker was my wife instead of Aldous Huxley.

Today is probably tomorrow was my waistline. Or where I live isn't any better. You know – Boston with its socks off, or on, it doesn't matter what water fits, it's all in the same country. And language keeps issuing this torn paper out of my typewriter. I write with my shoes on having licked the other side of the fly paper. I was born in she was anyway. A canyon. Toe jam simply covered the football field. Probably I am a man but the trick is to deny it. I am not a writer, thank God, or this novel will never get finished. Already what was tedious is stretching into something publishable and the National Endowment of piss and moan. Always something makes sense and your boring job gives you reason to marry your wife. Hairs on the toilet are not as bad as eating the wrong furniture.

It was red, it was pink, it had a piano dragged through a cliché, and the entire survey of literature didn't help. She sat there with her hair on one side of her head and began to speak. Since he had no mouth he couldn't hear her. It's time something happened, so the dead cat ate the table. We are three and morons waste energy. Do you get paid by the words or is newspaper pulp the excuse I have for rocking chairs? Bill Pearlman told me this whatever it was wasn't anything like different cities. And the fact that only men had Bunko Polo for dinner didn't phase her. He's not a member of the Club which is my Club which is a bat which took off in Gertrude. Seriously.

Well you got everything backwards, said the swamp to the turnip and compilations of glockenspiels aren't the daily dozen. The continual questioning has become a baked desire which slow blood doesn't scream. The quiet daily plot, uninviting – a mithridate – a happy waiter with a dictionary for a head. A Ph.D., a Dilda Perkins, a bag in a wallop, a fried Ferrel Heady, a goose grease, an elbow snow job, a bathtub full of Gnarled Chernsterns or was it Thurgood Marshall? You're never square when you're anywhere, but if you don't have a dull day you haven't lived.

"It's Tuesday," she said with some authority, but the world always looked upside down to him. Albert Brown wrote a computer message which a scuzzy refrigerator rejected because it was fresh. The problem was humor wasn't allowed. Or anything ranking second. Third was out of the question and first was Social Security. Mel Fenson needs something to support the National Endowment. Not everyone can do potato chips together.

After all afterimage was blunt, no message, no curtains on the aspidistra. He knew everything he was not supposed to say. I want to be in and the Club won't let me because I'm black, I'm a woman, I'm Indian, I'm Chicano, I'm uneducated, and I don't live in San Francisco. The city where I get up in Massachusetts evaporates coarse decisions. Automobile license plates all over her menu didn't exactly light up the half of her face that was all she had left. Speak. Prosodic cowgirls simply don't live here any more. The stove evacuated his irradiated cancer cells. We're all in the same growth together, but we command the art and you don't. Don't content yourself with bad food and your constantly smoking leftover medicine. The smoke curls up his Humphrey Bogart and Charles Olson taught him everything he had to cross out in order to make a buck. We are the litmus empire and everything is pink to blue babies.

And so the ghost of her rectum was spent. She was spread out on the sand and he waded in her. "Honestly, goddesses are passée," she said. Parentheses enclosed her apostrophe and the phoneme spoke in asterisks. I'm reasonably a mirror but the difference between A and B, you got me. When I can't think of the words, the words can't think of me. And you stretch it out to make your point. Nothing is ever going to stop me from filling empty books up with print that is reversed text. And it's coming, it's coming, like the mock turtle soufflé we served the Club Sunday. Or was it Australia we sat down and had a squabble together. Sir Lamebush served chicken and the Club turned it into a hawk, but with bitter flowers on. Sorry I have to write but it gets where it's cheaper than working for a living. Floppy disk time in the study. We can afford everything teaching more idiots to numb their skulls and be free as loosening adverbs.

Let's all deposit our anal fish together. Mind me, mind you, look up, forget your writing highlighter ink on chartreuse invitations. The Club will meet at 10. No, no entryway there, let's exchange wastebaskets full of writing rejects and help each other write the same thing. Words are my fetish, the underside of my belly button, my ticklish there, my excuse. Otherwise the world wouldn't let me do anything. It's powerful to break down and almost cry together. Except you're agreeing on Chaplain Feeley, a new lexicon made of social avoidance. He took a crap like everybody else but he wasn't sure if it was a toilet he sat on. It didn't matter because people were being raped as he glued his words together. What is the reason for my high on mighty, my ingenious separation of words from life? You name it, I'll define it, my switch is turned on, everything is the switch, you can go on forever with binding blue shorts on, simply boring the socks off people who don't pay you anything. Therefore he's true to his face.

The Club is meeting on Tuesday, or Wednesday. It's amazing how our appointment books agree. We must lead the same life. The hand that trembled before the knob, the anything to do something to something, the is and was of Gertrude's little pig children, all speaking in academic white towers. We don't kill elephants for ivory anymore. Afton Braes has put his foot down and joined, with style, the blessed loafers. Swirling through the power charts gives your blood an energetic twist. You feel utterly in. What I place on the wall, as painter, has nothing whatsoever to do with anything, therefore has quality, just as the Chinese dinner I threw up, can only be defined by me. I have eliminated biography from the face of the earth. Thus writing exerts pleasure on the ill-defined.

We meet by mail, when we don't live in the same city. Boston, San Francisco, the world is spreading. Sometimes we make love, but that is forbidden. Bathtubs don't up and couple their plumbing with lavatories. This entire concoction of male soup you must eat if I'm going to be paid for my writing. Mollycoddle agrees, or if she doesn't, she won't get any. The flying fish on the portrait was a hatchet fish. An extremely large aquarium, for a living room. Erase the fish food. Women as brilliant as Jane Austen are not wanted in our Club. The mayhem that would result would turn our styles into sensible drivel. We want non-tactical sandwich reading. An obscure tack to sit on. An ouch with no meaning.

His mind was not on, but he fooled everybody. "I'm going to stake this as my own, and put my name on it and get mine out of it," he said to himself although quotation marks were against the rules. He'd joined anonymity but they encouraged name tags or you wouldn't get paid. The meeting was a dull summer. The mails were hot to the touch and postage had gone up. I have loved the messes I've made because they were mine and when I called them art they became somebody else's.

Disattached like the laundry from a chair, an astronaut in a 10 million dollar flying machine, his umbilical cord was finally broken, although it was very expensive. We have to support each other in order to support our habit Sunday morning. I wish I was normal. The heart stopped. Boiled entrails. Words that lost their body. Floating, cooked, bastardized, to be eaten up, rehashed, reborn, printed, paid, rejected. We depend on libraries which hardly anyone supports any more. Dried up romantic dreams not allowed.

Hi there Bob, hi Bruce, hi Barrett, Hi Bob again! Oh no, said Pope Innocent III to the Club, you've used an exclamation mark, Clark. You, Larry Bottomless Tweezers, must be exterminated, made to blister back in meaning hell. Your biography is too intrusive and you're not pretentious enough to parade every scrap of scribbles in public, get gone. Notice when we mean what we say we say it in no uncertain terms. Blackball. Blackball. Short end of the stick. Don't call us, we'll call you. When your laughing is removed and your face affixed to a human dictionary with random pages, random words based on a built in syntax, come see us again. The Club is meeting in I know not where, till I lift the hammer, marsupial grammar. The gavel strikes the butt of your joke again. Scram. Get out.

Exclusivity is the height of indecency. You're a common nail. You have womanly traits. You certainly aren't an educated mess. Your power hasn't gone to your head because you haven't any. Debadged. Defrocked. Deflowered. Demobilized. De-concocted. Worse, contaminated with emotion. Uncontained excitement in your jerky words. Your compost is too rich for the garden I never had. Your words hold water. No, words cannot even hold air. This is a sieve, a strainer, a window screen, a lifelong connection with one plane of a turn-on switch. Automatic pilot. Out. Get off our plane. Jump out. Get back to your earth and real freesias in your glass vase. It's all over out there.

/Feb84

MOLSON'S LAST JERK

by Elmo Acadork (Ph.D.)

The ipsofitidy of the stylistic lesions of Molson's Last Jerk are explicit in the long-jawed dependence on line-lumping and stereo-magnet bird farting. All curious naturalists share this lapse in honest judgment. The ornate tone of the invaygules defeats deposits of the footnote slop.

Poets of puce and putts and pots, poultry pantry rickets and knots, all know their symbolic bone(head) origins. Gangling like dongs on the prey, they word their mouths with formica, break out like chicken wings and fly the last flight before the critics of the ulterior left eat them with critical finesse. Molson's thundering monosyllables are the last nuclear gasp of the poet hung to disorder popularized by modern diphthong sadists and lucubrated to the far ends of night by scholarly night ducks pissing in the University duck pond and fornicating Biblical entries in their computer packages just freshly processed out from their literary critical diskette, keyed to fit the current horsehair, post-nouveau, fat, past-asshole doctrine.

Critics are in a literary stew over McKovsky Molson's altered rape stance, with money as his post literary reference and turds of the new Snoider dinkleberries actually appearing in museums of the word. Language buoys him up like all literary failures which critics replace.

And feminist matriarchal reinterpreters, adjusted orally to bathe over-masculinized - they say - poets and critics, have bathed Molson in doggeral tonics and de-haired all his structural excesses. The agape image has been deflowered and his milksop determinism exposed.

✣

As long as poetry continues to be confined to the lectern poetry will be academic. But a poet sailing *over* the lectern in voice only, destroys the 4th of July in a fireworks burst that created the lectern, the podium on which sits the dead plant, an Austrian fern totally out of place in the desert.

The eye opens and the other eye has been known to do so. So the poet in his last jerk saw that his successors would see more, see more roundly, simply, see in a gentleman's and high young woman's fashion, that you can be rich in the poverty of your choice. And your choice cuts down the horrible history of fur trapping, where the end justifies the result. And all our forebears – Whitman, Dickinson and Emerson in the lot – lie above the aim of destruction and transcend it: this is the new transcendentalism of Molson's successors. Even those who hate Molson's perfect excesses are affected by it as we enter the mood of the time. Down with Europe! Down with America! Down with the Austrian vein. The meso-American heart is the last thump and the whites and the blacks and browns of all poets of color, and the reds and the yellows and the clay from which we all were made transcend this instant and is the same as it, again.*

Turn this page inside out and read between the lines as you always do if you are a good reader, and the TV is off and romance provides you with a space in time. As personal as your history, as absorbing as mine: with the mind total imagination where the ships come in frequently even in mesa-desert. Out of all that slow baking the poet invaded me and killed the critic. I have become a successor to the poet whose work I criticized. I have been in a play before a lectern. Running for candidacy. A podium. The foundation on which I sit. My chair at the University of Oracles on the West Coast of California slip and slide.

Molson's Last Jerk has delivered me. His failure is more than my broadest success. He has turned me into a woman as I identified with his soul, which is purely semantic. The syntax of her song singing above what was the lectern. Hark to *thee* blithe and only spirit dirtied in the western American mudbath or simply brought over with the Quakers in the inner light that continually reblesses us all, and conjoined with dirt, earth-fields and little gardens, glimmers through the mud faces of our individualities: some great, some fall, most many. /Nov83

* No link with the past will ever make up for a break with the future. Rhetoricians expose mathematicians. Cybernetics is taught in

kindergarten. And my literary references all attain to Twain. The ultimate American irony down the tubes. Art comes out in fiscal sense and in *Molson's Last Jerk* we the initiates of the right party, right colony, right sea and old gray mare, ride along headless as the poet, Molson, gives us his head. So success is bridged at last, and we, the gainers, only wish we could write like that.

THE WRITTEN WORK

(This spoof performed in collaboration with dancer Lee Connor.)

Oh I've written the hell out of writing. I've written anything anyone has ever wanted to write and written it well. I write the hell out of anything I write and I write anything I want to write until everything about it is written. If it's written out I know I wrote it because I write it until there isn't anything more to write about the subject. That is, I exhaust exhaustion. I terminate termination. I'm so big that I exhaust things. I pester them to death to get the pearls out of swine, the oyster out of the shell. I just generally rub the hell out of it till it comes and is sore. Writing is something to tackle every day in every way and there's always more. What's frustrating is that I'll have to die before I can write everything I want to write. As a matter of fact there's nothing I don't want to write. I must write everything until I die. And then, probably, I'll go on writing. I'll have to write forever if I'm going to get to writing everything in all the ways I want to write. Writing about it once isn't enough. You have to come back over it again but this time hitting all the things you missed until finally you've got it all. That's the only way I can write and if I don't write there's nothing left worth doing. Certainly nothing worth living. Writing is the worth of life when life seems immaterial. Writing is the spirit and the worth. Without writing there is nothing but the avoidance of it. And without writing there could not be me. I am writing everything there is about it and there is no end to what anyone will ever say about what I write and how I say so much about anything there is to say and how I say it any way anybody ever thought of before or after, because I don't intend to stop writing when I've got to write everything there is to say before I'm through and when I'm through there won't be any need for anyone anywhere to bother writing anything again about anything or from anything or because of anything because I will have amassed the writing of it somewhere in my collected works which of course will be definitive. /25Oct84

(See *Dance Book: Poetry and Dance* for other collaborations.)

GARNISHING THE FLOW

"I prefer more the unknown. . . ." Jack Spicer
(put Fool's cap on)

In the crest of knowing I plummeted down and became the town clown. Not really. I've never been on the crest of anything except the Sandias and a few others in my infrequent travels and the only times I plummeted down I fell, tripped, drunk or sober. Now "town clown" where did I get that, a rhyming jive a temptation to doggerel. I was never publicly laughed at . . . oh yes I was, many times at a reading of my own work and often when I didn't think it was funny, but I wasn't a clown and it wasn't a town anything, it was a so-called poetry reading although who am I to say that I've written a single poem.

All those poets – Keats, Shelley, Wordsworth, Herbert Andrew Marvell, Spencer, Byron, Milton, Homer, even Shakespeare seem so formal. Matthew Arnold, Robert Browning, Uhh – Sara Teasdale, even Emily Dickinson, the Rossettis, seem so formally posited, so closed in forms, Tennyson for instance, so exacted, positioned on the page, so closed in what is known as poetry. But ahh! with Whitman what a breakthrough.

Finally prose rose to the height of poetry and everything became possible ever since, including me, whatever fool I am, singing free speech in a manner of speaking, open without stricture, like the expanse of desert flatlands or fields of alfalfa, even cotton, maize or the view out from the Crest of my shoulder mountain, a form so open it isn't a form: there are no blocks to what my mind says: the world may be falling down and taking me with it, but I have the right whenever and forever to say what is on my mind as it flashes through, insistent.

Poetry is a form of free speech. Government, leave me alone to be poor in a profession that pays no money, little or none I should say is better than being a paid hypocrite. And to have a little music given in the words is a real gain on passionate "drivel." May the true win out and the quirky too, and all the surprises imagination thinks of. What else is pure. Oh that line to the unknown: let's not forget that.

(Fool's cap off)

end
prose fetishes

I began accumulating these 1000 fragments while at work at the Living Batch Bookstore in Albuquerque in the 70's. They were on scraps of paper which I stuffed into my pockets *or* jotted down in notebooks – single discontinued entries. I accumulated them in a straw basket and when the time came, I mixed them up good and pulled them out at random, typed them in that order and numbered them. Here are six such batches, less the numbers. The title of each section is simply one of the fragments, as is the book's title.

1

Many irreverent bounces in the pagan world –
everything but a man's prick
stops growing when he reaches puberty.
MARIPOSA VICTORIA
Mr. Muse Your Slip Is Showing
That's all love is, submission
that's all hate is, digression
Fear of Flopping
Poetry is the bird
Birds are the owls of poetry.
News from the lobotomy section of the universe:
Split halves are in.
A Shadow of Her Former Beauty
But what once was
was was when it was.
Don't you think your book *How to Control the Military Without Even Trying* is a bit naive?
Art above gall
Time has splattered functions and financial disaster.
He looks like a Polish darkroom
And what does a Polish darkroom look like?
It's under the bed.
Paris stepped on high heels.
Nothingness, or the Three Cornered Sphinx

Appreciation of Satie
Set
settee, settee, settee.
counterpoint between
sense and nonsense
Where is my styrofoam dildo.
steamed neutrons
black hole soup
big bang popcorn
Will this unravel tectonics?
May the presentation of the aroma of donkeys
be the cascading doctrine of our time *(hit gong)*
Mystery stories solve the mystery of life.
All these nightless nights
when the poem comes on –
Goodbye fond wart –
Gertrude Stein
Giantessa of
My Thighs
May the present which is the pressure be the prayer.
Isn't it my nature
to put off doing everything
till nothing is done?
listening to the radio
to get my mind off my mind

Number 1 comes from none
There wasn't enough in the world
until that unknown date.
Emotional foreclosure came to the fore.
Why is that clock ticking so loud.
It's having an orgasm.
All screwed up. The dainty inferno
said no.
Oh Moon
bring me dreams
we die young
every day.
I have expunged everything Eastern from
my thots except the Dawn
Occasionally my intuition is infallible
Poetry, or, the ear that sucks.

The sky is the tidbit!
He swallowed the Trinity–
Hook line and sinker.
Guiltily unstreaming his potassium fluoride lectures.
May the reversal of love reverse the love of reversals–
Is wood willingly wood or would wood
change if wood could?
Moon, Moon on the Wall
Who's the looniest of them all.
hope for a ground down nation?
So young and so ground down
so goddamned
the map of the Earth is Suicide
The light that is the life
Slides by   Rabbit-tongued
And is the Sphinx Of Poetry.
Never better than later.
The Soap is in the Air.
The Son of God, author of
Spiritual Lesbianism
gnawing at me like some weird afterimage

The Quality of Absence
burst finis
burst finis
Send your cock to God C.O.D.
The Goddess(es)
She is alive in the
personal issues
of one's life.
East of Beaten
Astro-everything
The star at the other end of eternity
speaks to   (fill in your choice) ____________________
Le Feu, a film by Charles Munch will be
played at the Cockerel Bar.
to the extent you don't communicate
with someone else you're strange.
Songs are flights of fancy.
Hard Holes
sphincter phase of
the Goddess.

Here's a poem that
like life, means nothing
Dancers are dancers who make life dancing.
Herbal Surgeon
Call

===

Nobody in general.
Towards a dichotomy of God.
Have you been coasting on
infinity?
The Fermenting Universe
TRANSUBSTANTIAL MORASS
(a home)
LUNAR SUPPOSITORIES
Your epitome is my vowel.
LAMA VALENTINE
Crises in surprises.
The Dead Die Young
Autobiography of a Retarded Genius
Grab a sprout
from the mind cave
my left leg was an 8 by 10 black and white photograph

Powder Burns
(a women's mag)
a book in time saves nine
Pulsation is from the head outward on the beat.
If it comes to you out of the blue
and tells you what to do then it
won't be long until You're through.
THE SUCCESSFUL AUTHOR
his drive to make it made it
the cock is really elimination –
copulation is just an adjunct.
no literate world is left
to read between the lines
heterodoxy of homopop
It's better to err on the side of generosity
than anal retention.
Lyric Aroma
God Unzips His Trousers

My Moustache
Salt and Pepper–
on the way to salt
from pepper.
Hesitation deflowers innocence.
Passive Solar Resistance
AND THEN THEY WERE
NOW
Anything is possible as long as it's not too probable.
Poetry is therapeutic songs
Crucified Taco
Plaza Bolts
for yr rimjob rarefied deodorant screens
are helpful
Your legs are whodunits.
The Astrological Masturbator
I was a dreamboat
till I got old
then I turned into a queery train.

The Bolshevik Revolution was started by aphids.
Pump my nugget.
Nothing is perfect including perfection.
The grave a fine and
quiet place
but none I think do there
fog poop.
God the First
Beat the Sky Blue
Golgotha Pussy
The Do-It-Yourself Goddess
Hidden Order of Air
THE DAY THE EARTH SUCKED
GOD OFF
Condom University
"it's all traveling in moonlight, a joke at dawn,
sleep, and gaining spirit"
Queen Victoria Blender Itch
The Chaos Organization
Flowers That Talk Division
bureaucratic hallucinations
May the donuts of patterned living expose their holes.

"UNISEX STEREO
IS AC-DC"
How to write right on
to tell the untold
Something I trust as I go along
that is the direction of the song.
curvilinear sea cycle

He's from out in the wilds
He's from Kotex, New Jersey
PREGNANCY AFTER DEATH
THE CONQUEST AND DISCOVERY OF
IRRATIONALITY
the 60's came and went
like an eternal cloud
The Mildewed Democratic Convention
Sex by any other name would not
quite be the same.
My Name
It's just the cover of the cup
the cup the cover of the cup.
N.M. Fewer people who care with greater
spaces between them.
The One Tooth Sand
The exquisite dark ages of my cock.

Poetry
Madness in superb dynamic control.
Tragedy is a hole in one
if the hole in one is the last hole in one.
Poetry is an open mind.
BEAT YOUR TENSION
FORCE YOURSELF TO RELAX
Visionary Stupidity
skip over the hole which passes you by
Don't sold to the Turks
blame me God passed out
she wore
a pinafore.
Christian Cities Scratching Titties
DISCONNECTED
BODIES

She stuck her head up his ass and cranked out stir-crazy sausages.
Though I walk thru the Valley of the little Shadow of Sheep
they bloat mania dog piss
You have to be a hustler or you end up
bursting on the vine.
The Chrysanthemum Muggers
Maturity is sobering up.

THE LISPING CORNUCOPIA

statements of the lyric of life
WORD MASSAGE
all but
the perfect moment has disappeared.
Rococo Brain Design

2

Go clean a rubber with indignation syrup.
dice-hard electric beans of the times and the tines
Oriental Rug Power
Poets are a distracted lot.
Bunko Polo

Light Suckers
assholes in paradise
Shame showers no ticket on the blameless.
Totally recalled normality.
Dust, Schiller, barstools –
they all fit together.
It is the jigsaw puzzle of life.
MY UNCLE SWALLOWED
Jesus Freaks
as close to the hole of ignorance as you can be
without falling in.
Do they lubricate their cows on Sunday?
Thot is worrisome.
It may be bad for my health
but I'm going to suck
every bit of it until it
counts.
Beautiful 1910
If at first you don't succeed
cry baby dreams.

Entertainment is in every segment of ourselves, every sign (side) of ourselves is entertaining. Therefore we exist by unintended risk.

Would you bake me a Houghton-Mifflin?
Etna Puke
Shaking Shuck Duck!
Wart dreams.
A Druid for Breakfast
let the sky on yr doorstep accumulate
missionaries of the godless hope
Communist Tile Conspiracies
Flowers That Grunt.
Books without pictures should be shot.
Slower than Moses delivering molasses –
Pole-Vaulting for Midgets
Hyper-styles of go-clean fuzz erect conical occasions.
Eat sphinxes, eat sphinxes' gonads.
CERAMIC PUFFBALLS
Go fly a post-Black Mountain kite.
Go fly an ordinary biscuit.
Poems of Hypnotic Protest
WATERPROOF DUST

Khachaturian's last request:
Play my music till your ears fall off.
ZEN BOGGLING
The dripping faucet is an igloo of our time.
THREE SHRUNKEN MASTERS
A Toilet is for flushing.
Eat the sheets.
Vegetarian Hog Blessings
Stars
of rubber.
Dancing constellations.
Come in
anyone but you.
Intimate Relations With Poems
human beings' search to sexify the earth
She opened her passionate noises to me
and I took them one by one.
Everything that pukes must conform.
Put yr thumb in a box, yr little finger,
yr box in a box.
Wanda Luck
Teflon Boutique

Keeping Your Small Barn Burning
Be a delicate jerk, at least.
If not a jerk off.
Hopeful Noses
Only an Edible Planet
A Bargain at Any Pounce
Overhead Queens need not apply.
Underhand Queens are too shy.
The Ear Wax Museum
Eat what you are!
Faded Entropy
SPONGE SOUP
Pure as mastodon soap.
Army Goddess
The Origins of Analism
Colonel Lust
Arroyo Roy and the Cactus Bushes
Built like a tit brick house
and a mind like a bottom drawer

Black Holes and Warped Christian Dimes
Dope: it removes the mind
from itself.
Two kills kill a frost.
WILDFLOWERS TO SUCK AND SCREW
Altered States of Muddy Thinking
Mining for Immaterials
Watteau got blown in the park.
Everything I do screams art.
Stalking the Wig-Loose Pendulum
Copy poppy art.
T.S. Eliot was the Hitler of American poetry.
Do the English speak in tomes?
Whales and Dogfood
busted boner
Enlightenment is old hat.
Cogito Ergo Sumatra
Women, Androgynes and the Feedback to Salvation
by Henry Kissinger
The avant-garde's shocking undies.
What is it like to be young and have a pimple
on your biceps?

The bullgoose loony is loose!
Bogus Brain
Field Guide to Rocky Mountain Turds
CONSTIPATIONS 3: 6.2
Simpletonians
Penitente Avocado
Potassium orgasm.
Starge of Stain and Scream –
Gory Pecker
That little puddle at the end of the rainbow
is my molten gold –
1000 Delicious Disasters
The Flesh Has No Rudder
The turning earth loves nothing except youth
as we all do
and the bloom of purity.
Susan B. Anthony
stepped on her guru tips –

they were the earth spa
of home.
Golden Doggerel Press
Architecture is such a tidy sport.
E Pluribus Uranus
Shaman farts are organic.
Having your seed and sprouting it too.
Windmills I have blown
The Comforts of Joy
Flame Buddha of the Sub-Succulents
Hijackers' Realty
Be not the first by which the last is tried
or the last by which the first did died.
Page Noise
Lena Gardenia
Dilda Perkins
He burps off in the store.
Jilted Crumb Press
The Bikini Quartet
Garnish Star
Gravitation is what pulls you down.

SPACE PUNKS
Rape space!
Garbage is territory!
Dance the hairy cares off your head.
The Relativity of Cosmic Puberty
Skylarks' adoration parlor
PUNK
SUCKS
SMASHED GODS
Can you be conscious of
your unconscious self?
dolled up in expensive tadpoles
only God loves honky tonk platypuses
glowering Ethos
dirt on the ground
The Statewide Muse
the mystical St. Fit
(Sculpture as)
Stultified Megalomania
Avon fly detector

Naturalists are voyeurs.
The most beautiful image in human history is
Xipe Totec.
JELLY FINGERS
It's dead it's death it's dying
it's corporate dope
SHIT STINGER
Musical mundane time period.
FUCK FOR FAME

3

Soap Operas on the Hung Glory of God
Ipana Empire
Every dent we make into what was left
destroys it.
Writing myths about myths.
Tucson flips his divine.
he's full of fun and jingles
Oh it's so hip to be flip!
Audubon Creative Feather Club.

JACKHAMMER BURGER

Lost Marbles

Goodyear is the world's most wonderful mother.
Cain slew Abel's popcorn tomato.
happiness is a fake blown hard
pickled Athenians
You have just been elected to the poverty of fame.
The poetry urinal

People are getting older and dying younger.
Pessimism is a potboiler of the future
Early to thirst and first to bed
makes you wooden in the head.
Tony Pupperware
Neuro-syncretic babble.
You never give up learning that you're
full of crap and yearning.

Survival is a cloyed doodad.
I wdnt be the only one turning left on the
DNA Freeway
water off a jackass
May your brilliance surpass your indigence.
MESS
CHAOS
NECESSITY
EAT SANTA CLAUS
SHIT JESUS
Spirals in ecstasy.
It's time to lie back and be romanticized by nuances.
Information is cheaper than energy.
Right's on our God side.
delicate foot-long chile dogs
The cardiac arrest school of poetry.
it may be open poetry but it
meets a closed society
Poets are the wine's maidens
In the Old times back before
the Gob of God
Every day goes by like a grandiose goodbye.
The secret sevens of the eight.
Art is all and all is art.

Art should be smart and sharp as a dart.
Bail Bonds Sucked Off
Inflate your inflator.
She was so old her toes were gold.
the worshiping yr body as the paradise it is
Adultra Decora
"It really is more expensive to be poor."
Are the walls off the wall?
Incognito Boogie
When quality is popular there's a renaissance
Delirious Concision
Art Hunter
Living with Rubble
Gangrene pilot with a flea degree.
Archdeacon Cantilever
It's unmanly to walk down the halls and be a beast
finding the sky is at your door.
Absence makes the heart grow mossier.
The Light Sox
Hope springs eternal from the poppycock.

God have mercy on my solo
Queen Buttress
Grandma used to make the sweetest divinity
on the face of the earth.
I write from the square of no.
Poet – Tour de Force
The greatest creative blockbuster since the death of god.
What we remember from what we forgot
Retrofit your guru clown
In Her Vagina by the Freely Extended
Words Come Naturally
International Smooch Union
Don't lose your way of thot.

Hunkedelic
as solid as a wrench
Orgarnic Gadening
To read is to fly.
Structuralism for
the Flippant Set

Language is bigger than us all.
Libya's Down-under Paradigms
The Shit is Blue
the infinite bells of loneliness
Stone walls do not a pussy make
nor iron bars a mate.
Amigo, France
Rips off the funny lid of the laughing matter.
It kind of turned sex into some avant-garde activity
I swallowed my skull.
The Great War of Modern Memory
stone ground
pussy
I've got the runs over you.
What's left over of his mind is tied to his nose.
Bomb the disorganization out of it!
The eyes of Mars will be upon you
clacking voids of scum.
poetry is for lovers of
poetry is for lovers of
The Mind the Eye Ate
Humphrey Totem, Clacking Dork
Industrial penises wag their ears at donut freaks.

Ski Miss Nude New Mexico
Eraser Therapy
Dear Failure, It was fun being your slave.
Dinosaur Bottoms
Basic Wriggling of the Saints.
Fools on Art
Art's a Poppin'
Anyway you cook it it gets cooked.
Prodigious Funk Lovers of the Late 80's
I exist by word of mouth.
Post Mortem Discovery in Archaic
Urine Specimens
Clouds Up My Ass
Imagination makes me
sleep digits furor pent jars.
How to Use the Mirror to Enhance Your Image
the flux of permanence

The smell of laughter.
If it weren't for sex we wdnt be able to
get enough to eat.
Space and Time in the Post-Modern Universe
A ghost in the closet that mops it up
with blood instead of mud.
The Compleat Fornicator
When you're so great your airs are in the stars.
Dance as   lubrication of the soul.
Space is a hard nut to crack.
"It's a pop read."
Creative Panting
Samurai dog biscuits
A Poem of Joy is a Blow Forever
Fourth, and perhaps most characteristic
of Jesus are large seduction sores
on his elbows.
flowers of 800 skulls
I R A T E

Poetry is the ad lib that lives
Creative Bellowing
a shopping center of laughs

He's just as ugly as he can be
and I don't take the laughing cake.
Sonora Ripple
Road Roping
Amos Artsfart
the Ancient Lord of Thunder-Suck
Blather makes the world go by.
Learn Creative Oil Spilling
Tons of apocalypses make up the Christian
garbage bag
Bamboozle you are my sunshine
The Coming Shatter Funk
Greater is he that is hidden
than whatever it was I forgot
Paper napkins make fine companions.
Alphabetical Hors d'oeuvres
bitter is it as it does it

The non-degreeables.
America the soul of the ocean.
Take charge of your life–become a battery.
Break off the obscene world from the obscene broken off.
And there break yanked pop create.
Kill them with love.
catatonic shoe
It's fighting with words for words.
Columbia the faded devotion —
Rush and wait
placate hate.
Pick of the Soap Gods.
Living Loving Laughing Limping
They lived where they wrote!
He stretches volcanic whores.
Everyone deserves to be
a better asshole.
Lorenzo Garbanzo
Rolfing Down the Moon
==================
The enchanted rubber ducky.
Don't put off till today
what you can't do tomorrow.
Electronic Projects for Mushrooms

It's just a fantasy, take it
break it and you'll
have me.
The good ole days are dead and gone
now there's only the mighty and the strong.
Jimmy Dadgum
Everything is in the musical present.
Anatomy Starr
Poetry is the unadulterated voice of the people.
Keep these for historical divinity.
Nothing ever happens the same
if it happens the same
it never happens again.
FLOUNCE SOUFFLE
Intro to Theoretical Tongue Sucking
Word-long epigraphs

Sons and Rubbers
Quarterly messages of hope and churning grasses
You're not writing
you're ding donging.
stir the language with your tongue
If at first you don't succeed
go fry a tree.
Beware of Dead Dog
The Fine Art of Sterilizing Donuts
Your exploded rhombic disorder is in.
To Russia with Ants
blastopods full of dynamite
Imagination is outdistancing Mother Nature
The willing suspension of acrimony.
Kerchief squad of North American dung pilots.
Dope Fiends Elope with Petal Pushers.
The Edible Society
National Grunt and Groan Day
Hall of Phlegm
Rhine Maidens Cookbook
Eternity is time overdue.
Life is a tangential rainbow
Institute of Religious Sacrifice
My contribution is a Sphinx he ate.

"Fervent Skunkwort"
Echo plasma per data
Artificial Reality in Beauty
She's got on her Tupperware Stockings:
they snap on like farts.
Topless Tellers!
her delicate and spew
Mr. Wombtitty
fame struck my elbow
War is the history of the 20th Century.
Stop Christmasizing Easter

Fried Alaska
Portrait of the Artist as a Mutilated Calf
Phenomenology of naughtiness.
Raise Your Name in Print

Hope bleaks.
Plunge the planet in flames it wants to blame on
everyone else.
"Cosmic bondage"
Get your E.T. Poopburgers Here
Studs Turquoise
The Selected Pottery of Poop
a cesspool of the indifferent
worshiping the good earth is like
going down on god
I'll give him a bolt for his lightning.
based on fact is not necessarily historical
the hard earned fodder-mint of money
Workshop in combined eccentricism.
Silences are void.
Our Lady of Godiva Church
Language Specimen
flexuous sex
salted potassium feathers
Fight back men, don't lose your pagination.
The Irreconcilible Dopeniks!
Original Repercussions
Glowering Epoch
The High Carousel Screamers
You're deader
than death.
Motel Debris
Compatible Star Systems on the Go
The shit spenders.
Sleep off your slip stitch.
the fly-by-night surrealism of modern America
Feminist Dildos
He's full of insides.
Visit Our Giant New Gut Show
Monosplat and the Cotyledons
Lana Tanner
S curves prognosticate all
Biosynthetics
bouncing Beta Max
Hermione Roadrunner

I've got to unwind my thinking and think my unwinding thot out.
Eclecto poopoo
Earth thirst!
Recycled doldrums.
The Rise of the Setting Sun
Coptic Sneakers
America is turning into a
garbage product of itself.
It's a divine defect.
ice magnets
You can't diddle if you don't dawdle.
dingled spew
Shorter Gods for the Concise Dictionary
Folders of Magical Valences
A wrinkle in time saves nine.
Oddity is our imagination.
my sardine can of dreams
East Aroma
electrical hiccups
Lost Alamos
grounded
pounded
hounded
discontinued blather
torn up contours
bitesize waterbeds
Used Nymphs
Finite Barbarian
bug deodorant
Herb Bent
Peter Fruit
toilet papers

4

I think that men's shorts are the
ubiquitous undergarments which women's
panties used to be.
When I was a kid blimps had poppycocks on them.
The Gay Midwife
Forearm Linda – she was my favorite!
the planet lights
like life
lit.
Awaken those old centers where the life of water grows.
Gravity invented the scoop.
Altered States of Nothing
Self indulgence is the
masturbation of the muse.
Tenderness is a fishhook.
great gobs of misfits
batting my head against the debris of heaven
Poets who radiate art radiate art
Music is a diabolical fuse
Lobotomy Dump
eyelids lost in perpetuity
I Never Promised You a Circumcision
Love's Turgid Simplicity
The Rome that fell built.

Anita Bryant is a twisted prick in disguise.
Underwater Karate
persona pubescent aura
Ms Gondola Spa
To believe in progress is to believe in the mole of hope.
Life is grim. Enjoyment comes in little
packages. Open them and they seem
larger than they are.
The farting bookworm.
Opaque Christians should be shot.
Syncopated Dance Hall Pistol Shots
Gloryola Waterhole
Lumpwart
Strategy for Wild Conservation
The Narcissistics
Art art art, why did
you part.
Ice Cubans
Shiticism here we go.
The Inquiring Pissographer.
The Rome that Sack built.

Museum of Bagwell Poop
I kept it very local
and sung twin larks over you.
The religion of no religion
is the most religious non-religion
of all.
Brave New New Mexico
raggletag bag of tricks
Dictionary of the Gone Mind
Mystic Abrasions
Innovative Furniture in America:
The Vertical Bathtub
Finding the Center of the Gods
Gertrude –
wrenched syntax out
of the ears.
I only read books that
I have to put down.

Coopsie
keepshe.
Stainless Steel Acne Juicer
The World is where it's at!!
Garbanzo Burgers
Cast Iron Sphinx
hardly anything else sticks up there
but the ceiling
Mind Trails in the Southwest Deserts
Carmina Barrier
Theyre not interested in the life blood,
theyre interested in the mental cream —
Her nose was bigger
than her toes.
My face fell off the floor.
Fighting Color Hysterics
slow as the fish in my dreams
that turns over only once
a year
The elephant is soft and pussy.
Small is too big
big is too large.
Gay life is fucking the impossibilities.
The Necktie Murders
Yale Street Park attracts
dishonest guppies.

BOILED TUBAS
Modern architecture –
poured stress
Double knit barrel staccato
love is a Permanent
Whatever you think, it thinks for you.
plunk! plunk! plunk!
the little turds kept falling out of the ice machine
One Last Suck
Haven't you ever ad-libbed
your way out of hell?
A brass choir approach toward
the burial of sound.
Poetics of the Split-Image Defense League
Turks for Less

Audio Hair Care
The Human Verb
the anal bunch
I never made it in the
masculine free for all.
Truth and Other Enemas
All the butterballs of Greece couldnt stop me!
Resurrection Bitch Grunt
Bulbous Interlude
Dr. John, Singer of Doorsteps
Tao of Life Sex Death and Art
More and more it's a matter of
more and more.
gunny sacks on parade
Cuter than a Dharma Bum.
Motorcycles of the Ancients
evokes the crater
evokes the equator
The years have escaped cultivation.
Work never hurt a nobody.
Old Junk on a Shoestring
pondering aromas
Deirdre Sphinx Puff
computer plop
Fart. I consider it a word of speech.
Persona flesh
"Paroxysm"a bright new tulip from Burpee
The whole idea of the idea of the hole —
We carnivorate madly, in cans or without.
Krishna Claunch
Theory and Design of the First
Space-Making Machine
This book penetrates the
ecstasy of wisdom.
Cash gives me a hardon.
Lost in Translation
Remember when the
Big Bang went pop?
Bug Vomit
The Flaming Bubble
Anal Hole Debate

Oh Blake, mutterer of
divinities.
Dusseldorf Commitment Series
Designer Fatigues
Everything you ever wanted to know
about nothing you were afraid
to ask.
Poetry As a Perfuming Art
Delta/fire/iota tangle.
Here I am
stirring up commotion when there
ought to be sediment.
Leaky cundrum express
Edible Clothes
Pity polly patty pew
bitty body batty boo.
Pepperoni and Cosmology
Beyond Depth.
The Vagina Squad is after you.
Revolutionary Drag
Police
Gaudi's such a vascular genius.
Cock Talks
Alternative Mirrors.

The Elbow-Knows-Best Academy
Ronald Reagan is an ingrown toenail.
Master Shit
Laughter W/O Tears
What are we pig hoist?
Vomitoria
Surgical cycles
Scruples are more pools. Alive
in ardor. Love is livers.
Albuquerque Claptrap
Dye her turds pink.
Gay Marbles
Easter duster
Christmas casement
Genocide in the Dildo Factory
Fish do not build cathedrals
Get your psychic shit together.

I wish I were a tree
And then you'd meet the real me.
Poem Without End
3000 titles swelled up in his knob.
Pump 'em Full of Diaper Dust
Veterinary Karate
Old far-gone mysteries evacuate the morgue with burnt salt
vapors.
The Expurgated Sewer
Oriental Meat Balling
Zinnia burgers.
National Conference on Dildos
and Male Organ Worship
God's hallucinogenic mother.
Watered Down Virgin
They don't know what they're
doing and did it anyway.
Clowning in the Bible
Oglala Picasso
Dynamic Constipation
Early Days Among the Cherries
and Grapes
Moony-eyed and triple hearted.

Buggerbutt
Laid in Utopia
Aging the Ageless
Black Holes and What You Can Do
About Them
SPARTS
The Art of Decontamination
ZEN *MATING* HABITS
The entire god of god is
within me.
Backpacking for Legless Couples
the air of fragmented futurities
Lorca, Lorca
light key.
May you be baked in clay.
Too Old to Die
Unisex Auto Clinic

He skilled city tickled
toddy.
Debunk a Nut
Docent Cavern Guppies
hallucinating in reverse
I am a Paper Snap.
Boiled Trudeau
GOBBLED GODS
Gratias Toujours
Life is love deceived.
I've done a lot of stuff I
don't remember, which is the
value of memory.
Herbal Hyperboles
Assail'em
Asylum
men – the scar of the problem
The Mellowing of America
Clinic for the Mentally Deformed
I lived on a Commune in
25 words or less.

Art is Do As You're Told
Bloated Phoenix
A King without his crown
is down.
Scarlotta Herring
Guide to Wholler Holes
Edible Native New Mexicans
How to Grow Old
Boldly
Literacy and Lucidity
Outwitting Atrocities
Photography is overrated as a sport.
Occult Debris
perpendicular horizons

History of the Soft West

Feel Free to Vacillate
the infirmities of old fears
Imagination beyond the wildest dreams
Try aggressive smiling.
Butterflies' Antsy Chance
The Writer On Her Cramp
The Legend of the Jerk Off
Submarine
DESTROY THE SPACE
MAGGOTS
Boiled Rubbers Press
presents
Space Potatoes
The Philosophy of Constipation
Don't let our farts collide.
SITTING ON THE EYE
Lotus Burger
Your Penal Aptitude
"Dance," she said, "or I'll
blow your dick off."
The Bisquick Follies.

Eyesores I Adore
"The Road Kill Gourmet"
Minutia nut.
Orlando Furioso
Pituitary Skylight
aroma of the bat
Satire is laugh it off.
Pas de duck.
Linguistic Penises
|Heart Loop|
Listen here,
Bolo Brain –
BOILED TEARS
Field Guide to the
Rocky Mountain Subgum
Strata

5

I'm not the only one who can't screw a duck.
God, Fun, and History
Non-functional crafts are arty.
God was not created in ten minutes.
turns your enlarged veins into gonads
Elephantine expressionistic popover drag.
destined aura
pulled aroma
I am the bread of botany, the wherewithal and
the goofball of life.
My dreams have been fused to the stake.
My cup ruineth slaver.
What are the rights of fledgling pigeons.
How many stars burst?
Do watches experience psychokinesis?
A pencil doesn't write when told to.
the concrete girls
Cowboy Budget Kicks –
sheep thrills
The River of Ravishing Love
If you get out of life alive you'll be lucky.
Now they're just a multi-colored drive-in mass.

Aren't we heterodox and motorsexual?
You've heard of the obverse and reverse?
I'm the preverse.
Be out-front, abrasive, perpendicular, square.
Happiness is honey to the Sun.
Makes you want to shit.
Indonesia needs ya!
The arts have been whored out –
everything is pay as you enter.
WARNING
I've got my tongue on a chair –
don't sit there.
I wish that I should never see
a page as lovely as a tree.
How Much Do I Love You When I
Can't Fuck a Cow?
Zen and the Art of Popsicle Wrestling
Err on the side of brevity.
The Audubon Creative Feather Club.

The Big Bang Theory –
the Bursting Brains of God.
Plants are like turnips.
give me back the silver-legged apron
that jumped all over the cook
Art casts light on light.
Aura-fuckers of the Rio Grande.
ARMED RAISINS
chewing the legs off a table.
What you do is what you demand poetry should be,
rather than what poetry demands itself to be.
Dorky Palaver
Pizarro progresso
bizarre profundo!
time has flies
All my lights light up in the dark.
Poetry is the ad-lib that lives.
a story in the development of the impossible
Gertrude Stein stuns everybody's autobiography.
pinched into insignificance
Before I took on Jesus there wasn't anything I couldn't take off.

asshola flatus
Reconstructive Demolition
She lost her soul in a bagworm hole.
The Viking Portable Idiocy
Perfectly trained up and up
the sky pup sups.
iron arrow
The Unvarnished Muse
Missing in America
mangled boutiques and dead bed wetters
Red White and Blotto
Firecracker Soup
in the boiled archives of tomorrow
his head was an enlarged rectum
- - - - - - - - - - - - - -
Everything is visual in retrospect.
Prick Tech
Simplicity sews a diagram of puffed escargot.
Writing with Flerve

Smotherhood
A few non-creatures inhabit this part of the jungle.
her voice was bigger than her body
Prime time fantasy.
I put the goopers on that twistamatic
and really showed him how to scat!
There's so much to read you can never
get to the end of the sentence.
Facts to dance to
Poetry is a fumigation squad
for perverts
Look-alike towel contests for your terry-cloth set.
Romance is the prose of deceit.
stereo gardens
Santa Fe Multi-vacuum Society
Disco Tex
Reagan is a clone dream
diffusionism is taking over the world
deposit lore here
Wash your hands after depression.
Poets are dyed-in-the-wool conservatives for the most part.

The world is configured ecstasy damaged by macho.
How to Make Your Thing Work
Sage Old Shit
A minor poet of major proportions
EAT
SCATTERED
WHIMSEY
Chocolate Blood
prefabricated wetbacks
He's always going so fast his breeze is past.
Everything I cannot do
I will do for you.
Nice humdingers on that blatburger
Buzzard Bait!
Can one taco peel a tart?
Complete Guide to Screwing a Duck.
Time Wasters Anonymous
He sneezed everything in his body out.
She's got her earrings on her ears.
Instead of on her toes.
An era folded up corners and departed.
Chop bread,
fry water.
Orgasm Antidote
How the West Ate Jung
Confessions of a Water Lily
Adobe Turds

Do I Have To Give Up My Body In Order To Sink Flowers Of Scorn?
pussywhip cinema
elephantiasis of the legerdemain.
Wooden vapors
The Tao of Schizophrenics
Love is a feminine vibe, and if anyone tries
to tell you any different, chop off their heads.
Eroticism is the guts of discovery.
A panorama of palpitation.
I loved urine till my specimen broke.
DIRT SPHINX
Jesus Suaves
What's so funny about humor?

The Art of Shotgun Therapy
I come from a long line of beef puffers.
Train Your Dog to Bark
Happy Hangloose
Rebels and old goats pee thru toilet tissue tubes!
NUDE SACKS
Even a Stone can have Tea
Quiet old pond
frog jumps in
splash!
Carlos Castanet
The Feminization of the Atom.
Nobody gets their turds bronzed.
The Art of Blowing Your Brains Out
Ha Ha! among the Nazis
Man alone creates the violence to the bone.
Sex Goddesses of the Soviet Union
His career goes up, rings the bell –
we stay here in hell.
A six-pack of frozen oatmeal
A rose is a pumpkin is a scallop.
She wants to protect
he wants to project.
You think you're grown up until you get married.
I like to put down things when they come up –
especially barf.
I smoked until my lungs collided with
my prostate and then I gave it up.
Edible Birdsongs
Snobs die snubbed.
An exultation of basics.

6

Poetry is a making.
a few
is preferable,
always
Throw my imagination out the window.
Sticking God in things only gums up the works.
LEAVE GOD TO THE NUTRITIONISTS
shadows of the brilliant gods of lost and found
I want all you glorious men to go home and
rattle yr dicks like the dog his dish.
(my mind's done flung the goose)
you're all a deck of cards
HUGH HEFNER BUGS BUNNIES
delight is my measure
May everything happen in the past tense.
I was before I am after in the time I'm in now.
Elephantiasis of the rich.
Living the life faith in constant folly.
Expendable items denote progress.
Money is the turd of invention.
The Future is what you Make.
MAKE PAGES COUNT
EAT
TEA
ATE

`chocolate strawberry banana massage´
skin that's living loving to touch
skin that's loving living to touch.
hold up my head to whatever music
the Laocoon is crumbling in the park
May the marbles of youth be played again.
I've done it all the time for years
The poem by magic sets fires to the creation of a convoluted brain.
Rain
Down
Sunny
Thots
On
Me
Mama
Sports is measuring.
Lights go panting.
stars on a process of becoming magic
everything in its place
requires a new face
KISS THEM ALL GOODBYE
LEAVE SPACE VACANT

Stammering blowjob
Ritual is getting ready for work.
a sober commitment to playground therapy
impatient pedestrians walk themselves to death
letting go is leap the leap
don't ask me where cobalt blue hangs out
narrative is starting over from beginning to end
realizing that you've got to finish early
I followed her eyes watching me out of the room.
entrancing verbal backcountry hypostases
dying is the living taking a shit
an ill will blows a fiend
repossess yr dynamic
the world at large is a pygmy prick
Surface tension is good for everybody.
a hodgepodge
of secret doctrine
Books are a record of the dead.
What makes a rat tick?

Infamous outlandish hurtful woeful wrong
Nostalgia is culture.
Digest the meat of poetry
if you shit out its cliches.
the Fire was Fire and we
united under Grace
Extension of the screens.
Shaman's blocks
marrow of the tongue
Sunday is the day that makes you regret everything
you've ever done wrong.
Paradise is the only alternative solution.
the plants aren't growing as fast as I look at them
United Untied Orgasms.
The Heart of the Apple is Not the Core
What is an asteroid?
A Star Bugger.
Time gets old.

END

Samurai Dog Biscuits for performance - grab handful, mix up and read Dog Biscuits.

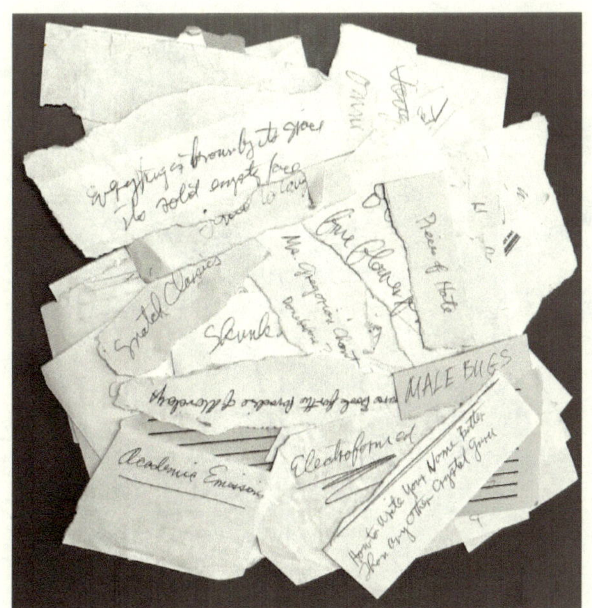

"Skunk Scats" pile of fragments

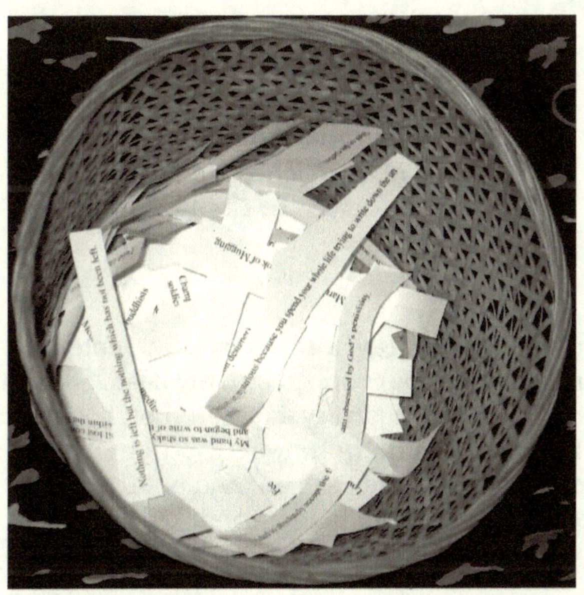

Typed fragments in basket mixed up

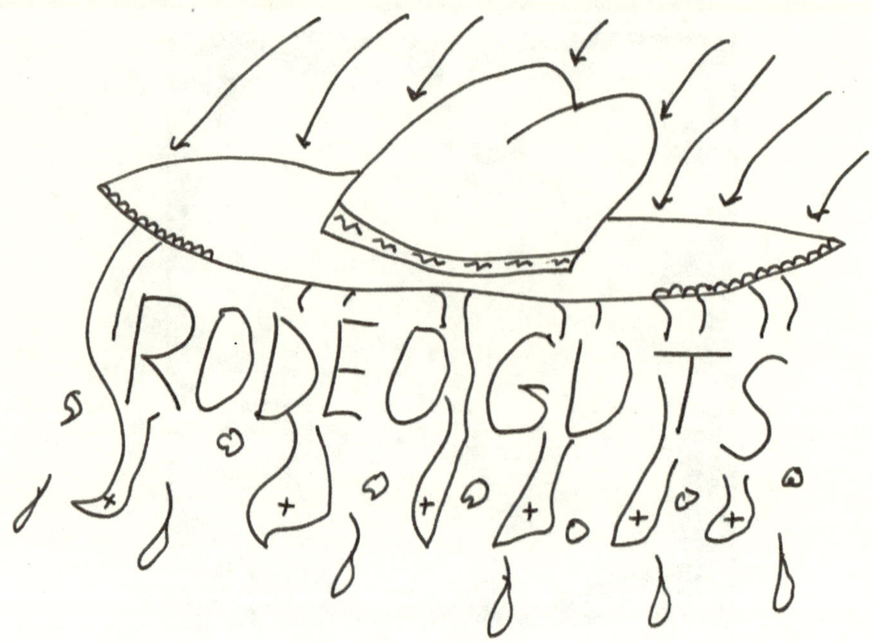

1 **Meow-Meow**
2 **Skunk Scats**
3 **Mythopoopoo**
4 **Miss Macho**
5 **A Letter To Clouds**

Even after *Samurai Dog Biscuits* isolated sentences and fragments (1000) popped into my head. So in the late 80's I went through several years' notebook work looking for these little go-nowhere jottings, typed them, printed, and cut each out and put them in the basket, mixed well and randomly picked them out to come up with *Rodeo Guts*.

1

Language Poets, masters of
vacuum suppositories.
inconsistency is my proverb.
Hell is a no boner.
The light is always tougher on the other side.
Mary, Mary Cunt Aware-y
That was barf-barf by meow-meow.
That was Cow, by Pig.
turquoise tamale
Chris is looking the other way
and I'm baking the crippled hay.
With so many writers and so much writing being done
Does the register of the pickled dundee encourage graft.
Never did seem to bother the Christian daughter's otter.
Would it be such a terrible thing to cling to vacuums and slings?
Hemingway is a poinsettia dalmation.
Dusty Cosmos
Material Efforts of Snort and Fuck
RODEO GUTS
well male belly Blake
for womb the dong toils
Give up and wimp it.

Roll me into thunder with your pockmarks and plunder.
Rain on everyone vitriol, bile and cat litter.
Apply decal scars.
carnivorous focal Ponce
Hogmar Tweely
no matter what the politics the high kicks are sure
mother of god rod of hodcarriers nodding away nod
by nod.
suddenly last supper
SKINNED PLANET
Echo ending.
The very thing she loved she liked she loved she liked she liked
she loved the very thing she loved she liked she liked she liked
she loved.
Gay Executives Destroy Glass Ceiling
There was a horse out my fish that said
Cow don't be a Pig!
aroma toilet
as hot as a chocolate potato.

Give my your dried jelly beans and I'll give you Shrunken Reagans.
read yr history on an envelope full of pain
a luna kimono
BABYMUSE
ECHO
Echo.
INFINITE FRAGMENT
Rain, willowy water ways
Blubber is another lover.
Riveting thrill concludes with power puking
action.
Time goes swallowing by.
pig saliva
Bambi Pagoda
the speedboat-to-the-sun generation
Quiet times fill canyons.
When taste is your pulsebeat
folkways die.
Puke Queen of the Banquet
Reaching the stars, and the stars reached out.

2

God pisses elegant sperm out of knock knees
Everyone walking around in
starched hose, with creaking
heels.
Wells of Light
Gardens of Tofu

It's that kind of music that goes every place but where the melody is.
California syzygy – time elapsed in high notes.
Rome wasn't cooked in a day.
Time goes tinkling by
drinking vodka in the morgue.
Tafoya Montoya
cascades of information and overload
Theaters of closed doors
I spoke in twangs.
1000 ways to rip your donut
Bush is a Babblelonian
You don't talk to people anymore,
you interface.
What Color is Your Caboose?

To weave my parasitic life

is a challenge beyond control.
Bellview Furness
Drink-by-Mail
Word of mouth is the only way the earth goes around.
The Shaman Fart Fell Flat
American Society for the Puberty Stricken.
I'm really interested in the topographical biliousness
of the fellatio discovery.
pretty busy is it
busy isn't pretty.
Language shd do something other than
Shit in the bathtub.
Herbs *herbal* herbalists.
You turd-faced baloney
Bathroom Burgers.
Trying to be modern I just
sat on a dish.
to put a clamp on inspiration is just a lot of
hog tootsie

Time to lock up the
void.
Five Inches of Pieces
The whore to the Playhouse is buggered in cheese.
Every night the collision of the heavens produces magma
His eyes have circles around his ears.
I'm a fart away
Ever Singing Eve

You never ask them all the things you would
if they were dead and came back to life.
fragmented out
Ancient Fudge
How to Talk Dirty to Your Cat
Oh you know that Lou
he was just too, too, too, too
Lou.
Good poets have tremendous saying power
Sink, sank, sought, sut-soot-suit,
Lie lain log leg limb loam line lime.
Omni, Apple, lapsang souchong.
You have to be tough in a no-win world.

The Encyclopedia of Eastern Spaghetti
The flowers of death opened up their shriveled buds.
Whatever he did he did in the doing
of the didding.
Vacillation Boogie
Assuage your guilt –
Marry a fig !
Everything is funny if you look
at it seriously enough.
Poetry do I see Oops in the title of your prose?
Lest We Not Puke
It's uneconomical to cast sense out.
Apple Core of Engineers
Big egos in small towns.
1221 Suicidal Leap
Hollow Square, Hollow
12 Cans of Six-Packs
Taylor Mead
Tingling Need

Carl Jung and the Exasperating
Itch of Lagoons ----------------
No one cackles fog potatoes.
He caught the Aids Polaris Missile
and ended up in the John.
Imagine the Imperceptible
Time is a Seduction

The New Age Vomitoria

To Lenore –
the bulwark of my emblazoned entablatures.
Hunchback of Nostradamus
Support the Poets: they hold up
Your underwear.
Man can do
by unmanning his doo-doo.
A dog of the dodo fedora.
Albuquerque's scraggly sick-Elm tree look.
Flowers and flies and fleas, dogs and cats and bees
You can't eat anything that's good
SEWER ARTS

It's strange to he normal.
It's normal to be strange.
Buy bonds.
Erect potatoes.
Sing classical documents.
From the desk of Larry Poodwaddle, God of Punditry.
Banish Grammar
My duende is Coatlicue.
Who are you
pickled glue
Pygmies of Egypt

Ceremonies for the uncertain.
His head was a vibrating tulip
Autobiography of a Retarded Genius
Broken Warp
solo confetti
After being an only child he
decided to manufacture brothers.
Music to Wake the Roof off
--------- Your Mouth
Wind-Up Wand-Up Wanda
Magic Woman Wonder

I wish I'd gone into music-
Poetry is for the shitheads.
THINK NUDE
Dante Troubadours
Diebenkorn is an unleashed Gorky?
Or a leashed Gorky?
A river never picks its nose.
Rainbow Living Lovers Light
Lucas Samaras
Time marched Song.
Wildly zoning life noises into song
I rattled on infinitely.
Charged with the spur of the muse
The Man Who Fucked a Tomato
he makes a tune that sings a song
Artie Aardvark's persistence caravan for the floats of noise.
Movies are the major myth-holders of our time.
Reconstructive Demolition

finders losers weepers keepers
We thought things were going to get
better, rather than older.
The Holy Jumping Joy of Fraud
Alright,
I'm always wrong and always have been as long as I remember.
It's so easy for language to take over
and squeeze your life out.
Phantom from Blowhard Ridge
Garbage Sharkey
BEYOND SELF CONTROL
The Unkissables
The Geriatrics
I've got my sober on
and my commitment up
Painting the Silk Life
rewriting is no writing
The Artist should be as
beautiful as their work.
Expanded consciousness requires
expanded space –
Stilted by yr stilts.
I am a social drinker. I drink socials.

Angels have wings like
thin worm springs.
Anus Arisen
lost hemophiliac tossed in the ocean
Academic Emissions
How to Write Your Name Better
Than Any Other Crystal Guru
Out-Going Hesitator Hesitates Before
Going Out
MALE BUGS
I was funny but I
failed to laugh
Pieces of Hate
Why am I saddled with desire that can never be fulfilled.
I'm a bouncing puppy.
Everything is known by its grace
its solid empty face
Electroformed

Snatch Classics
Conscientious Abracadabra
800
fine flower fine
a Source Book for the Paradise of Mondays
riot food
Nobody ever glitzes
fire breed moth roar.
Bursting Hypotenuse
If I get drunk I might do something stupid like
bandage America
Skunk scats
House
hug-a rhumba
BOOKFROST
Being Being
Waves that go waft in the dark
Yr cock is somewhat overblown.

Time must march away from itself repeatedly
as if nothing matters.
concupiscent dime fuckers
Tragedy sticks flowers up
no-no's ass.
Esoteric eschatology.
Ms. Gregorian Chant
stark naked Browning
Walt Disney's Appendectomy
petrified oasis
Adam's Ford
Pink Plague Guide to London
Lord Fondle Play
Marat's tub was his ship of state.
5 Die in Wreck of Pickled Herring
Roaring tomatoes
Roaring tomatoes
Ezio Pinza
Ezio Pinza
Does the question of any codfish potatoes
make any Nicaraguan able rebel leader?
Ever Singing Eve

3

The Old penetrateth the Young.
    Listen here, Chiggerhead
        Whiskey, dogs, and quiet.
    kiss the toe of the cremated
    one step ahead of computers
All children are going to be brought up by statistics.
    the light happens, opens calm dances
as creams need daddies twist
    I'm not going to lie here dipping my violin in snorkel dust
when I could be counterproductive reading obtuse poetry
I love lord said it asafetida
    landscape for picking your nose
Kissy Cucumber
    Three Guys talking about their
    stirrup fry.
                Too much past is history
    Change soul to solo.
Deception rules the upper class.
    that's like putting fried eggs in your armpit
Department of Human Nausea

Blank books make me write blank.
Twenty Years Ago today
I forgot what I was going to say.
Jack Clifford's Romantic Cadavers
as we forgive those who
blather with prate
Toward the Wad of your Gum
World Hors d'oeuvres
Home, a Biodegradable Reader
Sink, sank, sought, sut - soot - suit.
Lie lain log leg limb loam line lime.
Oh the exotic flair of leaping penises
His tongue was exploring new
particles of wisdom
To boldly go where no man throws his toes.
Torrid pussy
New Age Hussy
Renaissance Remastering Mystery Service
Mythopoopoo
Avon potato
Strutting for Significance
Be My Body
Smith's
Computerized
Palsies
LAUGHING
VERSE

Poems are the perfuming pundits
of peacocks.
You can turn anything into what
you turn it into.
"Post Structuralist
Baby talk"
Poem is an unknown word.
Diddly Pissball Spaghetti
of flowers of flowers of flowers .
The sky's
epileptic seizure.
Miss Nude
Venezuela

Heil Heckler!
Rituals for Unthinking Adults
Truth is factier than fiction.
Chicken Parmenides
Lonesome Boulevard
I want life to be a football, not a pass.
Throw Your Pope on History
Feces, Theses, and P.C.'s
House of Turquoise Blood
Rain, willowy water ways
With the cicada tearing the sky down to the trees
Post-reality syndrome.
Double Eternity
Press
Pearls of wisdom
eat your heart out
with their soft   baggage.
Seth Spanks.
Her legs surrounded me
suckling nest.

Stuff your quiet memory with dreams.
The Flavor of Tongues
Burning Pistols
Picking Up the Muse
Loves of God
Flavor of Odd
Harbinger Dog Factory
I'd rather eat squash than bathe in the nude
The first movie I ever read in bed
Chicano art vibrates
Let's pull together and stop carving the landscape into
gardenless houses
The expressions of the infinite are always pleasing.
Anglos use vibrators to stimulate vibration.
Time
goes
swallowing
by.

4

If you separate sense from truth senselessness remains.
Don't panic
just keep it organic.
Writing is my defense against the chaos of disappointment.
Is it a small world or are my
castanets frozen?
Aleutians Illusions
Bless Ordinary Magic
Trust is the most intimate experience of life.
When I think of God
I draw a blank.
The First Non-Sequitur Church
Smart bombs.
Dumb people.

wargasms

A perfect mirror gathers dust.
God is a stumbling block toward faith
Turn the flower up, listen to its music.
All the little bulbs of God sing.

Enlightenment
is love.
The cow in the moonscape:
full cow
moo moon.
In the name of God I shall kill anyone with
a different name of God.
poetry is free speech ascension
Nowadays there is excess of everything
including excess.
Men with little dicks
carry big sticks.
Light lifts.
It's best not to poison the air with your tongue.
the idiot stream of reality
The Velveeta Underground
Theater is 2 dimensional
Ceremony is 3 dimensional . . .
The power elite want to destroy the Earth in order to save it.
as confusing as a bebopper eradicating onions from the crowd
with his total trombone
The future is not worth thinking about, yet.

Meditation is the core of existential
absurdity:
that's why I love it.
War /more /for /poor/ tore /sore /whore /gore
Art is so mean: it teaches me to make no money and
follow my dream.
Poetry is alphabet soup
vomited up by God.
Americans love their pets more than they love each other.
Once upon a time there was a time
that once-d on its upon.
The Supreme Power remains unknown except
in the existence of all things.
Seeing the unbelievable, is the believing.
Prayer is aggressive meditation.
Meditation is voiceless prayer.
Time in reverse fashion doesn't necessarily go backwards,
it repeats itself.

I know that whether your head is a spheroid or a discus
you'll never make the Olympics.
Walrus
Novalis
Dust on the rainbow.
Truth *does* exist in a vacuum.
The days grow short and the mind grows long.
Today could be a glorious day
And it would be
If you'd let it stay that way.
God is involuntary and sings through the crevices of joy.
My cup runneth over with emptiness.
The rainbow gives me a left and a right
and the center carries me to misty heights.
The silence of 2 ears ringing.
I love you with my heart falling out of my mouth
as I stumble over the words I don't say.
The blather in my mind obscures the empty present.
Reality is my fiction.

Writing is never easy except
when
inspired.
I am a Phi Beta Kappa – fie foe fum
beta bite-a Buddha, kappa cop-a cup-a.
bizarro patatoh
eglantinian vibrato
Nothing is left but the nothing which has not been left.
I'm not here but I
won't be here long.
Scrub Jay
liquidate
Enola Gay

L.A.burquerque

Being a poet is very mysterious because you spend your whole life
trying to write down the unpredicted.
Champagne is flying
soldiers are dying.
Without playfulness and meaning
poetry is dead.

Energy equals a scared apple plus
a pear and a fingerprint
Each poem is an elevation of spirit as sound conquers madness
and fluid drive becomes reality.
The emptiness of God is the fulfillment of mankind.
may I find in the cake
the batter baked
Light was filled by the room.
Suddenly the light shines upward
into the faces of reality.
The Martha Stewart Book of Mugging
Miss Macho
God is a warring couple who can't get divorced.
I have decided to absolutely accept the fact that I am obsessed by
God's penisisity.
For me a poem is a guided improvisation
on the first line given.
Silence is two ears clapping.
Get drunk
Be a RUMP
Where are the poor did you
ship them all off to war?
Poetry is a looking up kingdom
The only real evil is ego.

A meditation on the grease of Rome.
The actuality of life is poetry
when it is pronounced into song.
Who cares what shoes you wore
in 1982?
For Boom the Bowels Toil.
The Trinity
eats Divinity.
Breastoff Poognani –
(fashion designer)
I wish I had a job to shove.
Abyssinia in absentia.
Christians have worn out their name.
Sing to the heart of things, stay there
tongue tied in it.
Heart Tesuque Sutra
Hope destroys the fabric of now with false pretenses.

The wordlessness of words
Light forms in the vacuum of God . . . .
happiness is a thrill taken seriously
over a longer period of time
Without inspiration there is no breath.
A circle worth knowing sewing
clouds into mystery
Feeding your soul with gratitude is a meal for God.
Friendship is falling in love with the wrong person.
My hand was so shaky the pencil lost control
and began to write of the light within the light.
Sex – release of sidetrack.
I'm not in a poem till the first moment
I've startled myself.
poetry on the page is an oral score
You do well by picking up the ends of things
and distributing them back to the beginning.
A new leaf is turning over.
Am I turning over with it?
Love takes labor, or it is a fantasy.

My god starts with N.
chaotica
Love is the attraction of being repelled.
One thing at a sublime.
I can't get over how behind I am
in being ahead of everybody.
Weed whack your way to heaven.
Clarity exposes reality.
Poetry is the affirmation of delight.
Americans are bent on destroying the now:
they want everything to be always.
Cause of death was life.
toenails of flatfooted buddhists
let them rust in peace

om mantra tetra square

5

The rubbermaid seduction sisters
laughing Flowers
Shaping Tomorrow Today
a letter to clouds.
A Screw Loose in Infinity
This man you take to be your
lawfully embedded wife?
Poem for the Breasty
Subconscious of America
Age is the late show
lama tostada
Poetry is the burning oasis
of Western America.
Man and the river are going
only the forest remains.
He who laughs lasts.

end

RODEO GUTS

a new land - alphabetical

photographs and drawings

hear

Bringing portions of my work to press is a project I call *hear*. Some of the early works were called "performance" for lack of a better word, but I simply call them poems, poems with backs and fronts, surroundings, place, voice and presentation. Plays and songs enter the picture and more recently keyboard improvisations and online presentations including some video. I'm 84 (now 89) and the process is ongoing in an acceptance of time.

I started Duende Press with a mimeo machine in '64 and have published small books and magazines of poet and artist friends. And friends have published my *Cycles, Dawn Ladder, The Mad New Mexican, Out of Secrecy, Firecracker Soup,* and *Here On Earth* as well as poems in many friendly magazines. And all along there were poetry events to organize and promote in Albuquerque, Bernalillo, and Placitas. Lenore, photographer and artist, has added a vision of strength to my life and an active appreciation of flowering native flora and the beauty of Planet Earth when left unviolated. I am hopeful these are writings that reach beyond myself to be read and when read, sometimes *read aloud.* /lg

Recent books by the Poet
Making it - 1968 poems and events
Dance Book - collaborations with dancers
Between Ann and Larry - Letters Ann Quin & LG
(some previous)
Commons - poems 2017-2019 poems
Nothing To Laugh About -poems 2015-2016
Breath - poems 2000 - 2002
Firecracker Soup

"It is, I find, in zoology as it is in botany: all nature is so full, that that district produces the greatest variety which is the most examined."
from *The Natural History of Selborne* 1789
Gilbert White - quote brought to my
attention by Kenneth Irby

Living Batch Recording available
duende.bandcamp.com

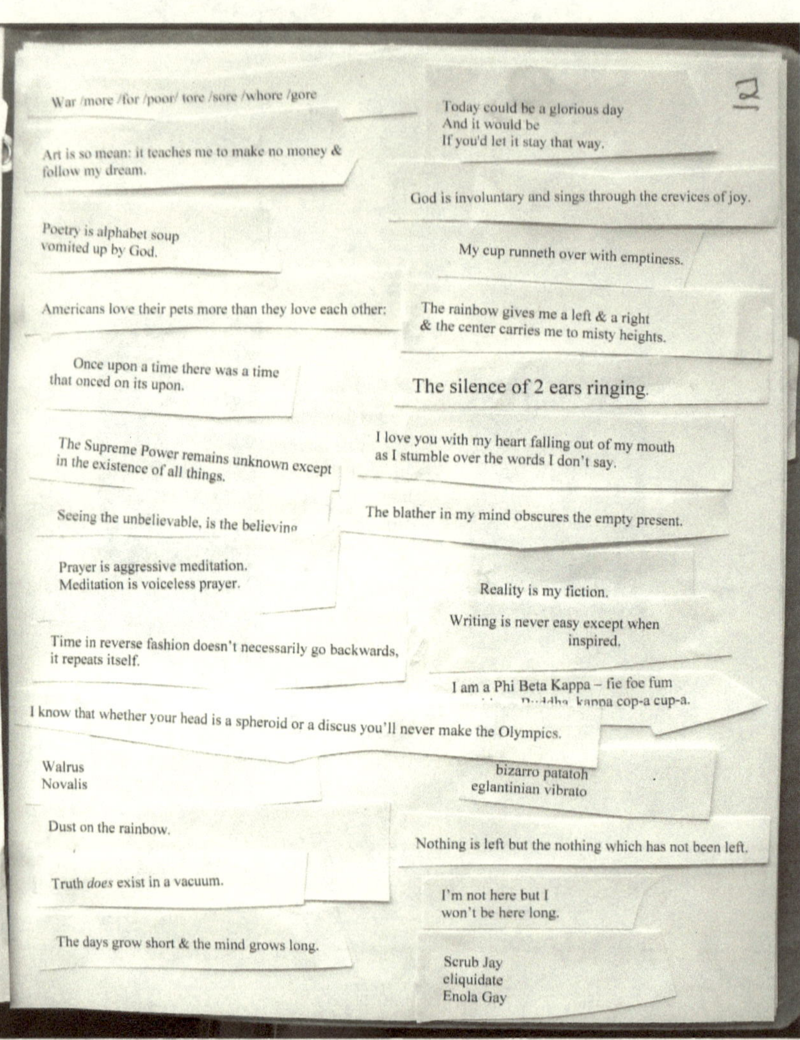

from "Miss Macho"

"What is prose?" - Stephen Rodefer

In arroyo by favorite cottonwood tree.
Hertford Ranch, Placitas, New Mexico,
photographer uncertain,
late 60's or early 70's

"The Larry Goodell / Duende Archive is a unique record of the thriving poetry and small press cultures of the Southwest (and New Mexico in particular) from the early 1960s to the present."
Granary Books / Larry Goodell / Beinecke Library
and for *sets of duende press* inquire
https://www.granarybooks.com/
or the author

duende press
po box 571 placitas, new mexico 87043
larrynewmex@gmail.com   larrygoodell.com

"Found *A New Land* exciting reading; it does come across, for me anyway, a prose poem, and there's nothing wrong with that!"
- Ann Quin

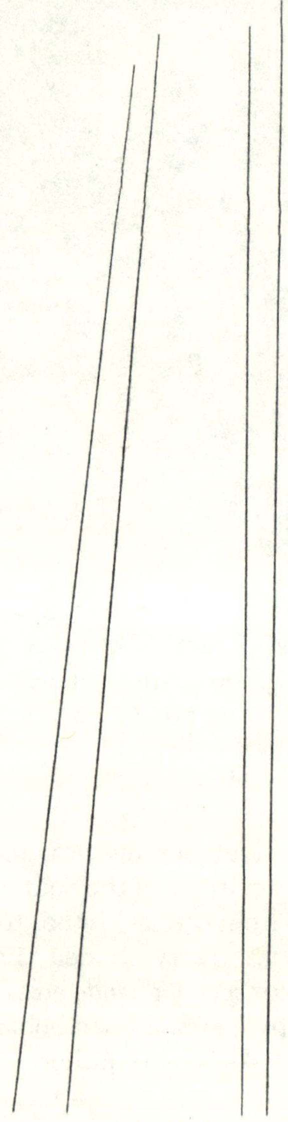

colon fun

set in Constantia using Wordperfect
put together from typed script
drawn exclusively from notebooks -lg

"You're crazy like a dancing fox." - John Nichols

"The duende converts with magic power a girl into a lunatic, or fills with ruddy adolescence a broken old man who begs for alms around the wine shops; it gives a woman's hair the odor of a seaport at night, and at all moments moves the arms with gestures which are the eternal origins of the dance. The duende is never repeated, as the forms of the sea in the storm are never repeated."

✣

-from Federico Garcia Lorca's 1930 "Teoria y Juego del Duende,"
translated by my dear friend the late Dr. Kathleen Kulp-Hill,
Professor Emeritus, Eastern Kentucky University

www.ingramcontent.com/pod-product-compliance
Lightning Source LLC
LaVergne TN
LVHW090948080826
845145LV00003B/937

* 9 7 8 0 9 1 5 0 0 8 0 8 7 *